Nick Carter made Mahbee get out of the tub, but he would not allow the man to put on his robe. It's hard to be brave when you're buck naked.

When they were standing in the bedroom, Mahbee's body began to sprout goose bumps and he started to shiver.

"You're mad," he told Carter. "My personal guards are right outside the door."

"Well then," Carter said. "I guess I'm just very lucky to be in here with you."

"You're the American."

"That's very good," answered Carter.

"Are you going to kill me?"

"Better and better."

"You can't!" Mahbee croaked, choking on the words. "Your country would never stand for it."

"What they don't know won't hurt them . . ."

NICK CARTER IS IT!

"Nick Carter out-Bonds James Bond."
—*Buffalo Evening News*

"Nick Carter is America's #1 espionage agent."
—*Variety*

"Nick Carter is razor-sharp suspense."
—*King Features*

"Nick Carter is extraordinarily big."
—*Bestsellers*

"Nick Carter has attracted an army of addicted readers . . . the books are fast, have plenty of action and just the right degree of sex . . . Nick Carter is the American James Bond, suave, sophisticated, a killer with both the ladies and the enemy."
—*The New York Times*

FROM THE NICK CARTER
KILLMASTER SERIES

NiCK CARTER

KILLMASTER

CARIBBEAN COUP

CHARTER BOOKS, NEW YORK

CARIBBEAN COUP

A Charter Book/published by arrangement with
The Condé Nast Publications, Inc.

PRINTING HISTORY
Charter Original/January 1984

ISBN: 0-441-09157-1

Charter Books are published by The Berkley Publishing Group,
200 Madison Avenue, New York, New York 10016.
PRINTED IN THE UNITED STATES OF AMERICA

PROLOGUE

Thirty minutes away from a violent death, President Bili Makumbo was making plans for the growth of his small Caribbean country, Santa Caribe. But, of course, he did not know that he was going to be assassinated.

Never before had President Makumbo been in such a position to obtain wealth and stature for his small island nation. As soon as it had become known that a large mineral deposit had been found in the interior hills, he had started receiving offers of trade. So far, he had been approached by England—from whom Santa Caribe had won independence a few years earlier—the Soviet Union, and the United States. With many other countries, both large and small, still to be heard from, he had nevertheless just about made up his mind as to which country he would deal with exclusively. The mineral in question was very important, he had been told by his mining people, in the preparation of special fuels, and these fuels were essential for certain kinds of military hardware. He did not really understand such things, for he was a simple man who had been elected to office as Santa Caribe's first president merely because he loved his country and his people. He had never claimed to be a great leader or a great politician. Still, once he made his decision, it would stand, for he was, if nothing else, a firm leader.

And that was why he had to die.

"Mr. President?"

President Makumbo looked up from his desk and found his assistant, George Mahbee, standing in front of him.

"Yes, George?"

"It's time, sir," Mahbee said. "The vice-president is waiting outside."

"Very well," Makumbo said. A slightly built man, as Makumbo stood he found himself still looking up to his taller assistant. Makumbo was not only slight, but at the age of forty-five he looked a good fifteen years older. He had led a hard life, and found the pressures of his office both emotionally and physically draining.

Mahbee, on the other hand, was a robust, powerfully built man of thirty-two who had served as executive assistant to the president since Makumbo had taken office. As well as being the president's assistant, he also served as his bodyguard.

Makumbo followed Mahbee out of the office, down the stairs, and over to the limousine that was parked in front of the Presidential Building. His vice-president—albeit in name only—was waiting inside.

Makumbo got into the car next to his vice-president, Jules Berbick, and Mahbee entered and sat on a jump seat facing the two men. When he had pulled the door

2

shut after him, Mahbee rapped his knuckles on the glass plate separating them from the front seat, and the driver started the car.

They were heading for a large park a short ride from the capital. There President Makumbo was to address the populace of Santa Caribe, who were eager to hear what their president had in store for their future.

Fifteen minutes from the Presidential Building, on a narrow road leading to the park, the limousine suddenly came to a stop, and President Makumbo frowned.

"Is there something wrong?" he asked, trying to peer at the road ahead. He could not, however, see over the head and shoulders of his assistant and bodyguard.

"Nothing for you to be concerned with, Mr. President," Mahbee assured him.

"I don't understand," President Makumbo said.

"You will," Mahbee said. At that point he produced a .38-caliber S&W revolver from inside his jacket, pointed it at the president, and pulled the trigger, effectively covering the rear windshield with the back of the president's head.

Then he turned his attention to Vice-President Berbick. . . .

ONE

"When was the last time you were in the Caribbean?" David Hawk asked Nick Carter.

"During that Pleasure Island thing, over a year ago," Carter answered without hesitation.

"Yes, well, this visit will be very different from that one," his superior assured him.

"You mean this time I won't get shot at?"

Hawk frowned at his number one AXE agent, then looked down at the folder on his desk. They were in David Hawk's office in the Amalgamated Press and Wire Services Building on Dupont Circle in Washington, D.C., and Carter knew that he was never "invited" there for just a social get-together. Wherever Hawk was sending him now, there was a damned good chance that he could expect to be shot at, at one time or another.

Carter, knowing that Hawk would get to the point in

his own good time, lit one of his custom-blended cigarettes and waited.

"Have you ever heard of Santa Caribe?" Hawk asked, finally rewarding Carter's patience.

"I can't say that I have," Carter admitted after a moment's thought.

"No, not very many people have, at that," Hawk said. "It's a small island country in the Caribbean—a new country, a few years out from beneath the thumb of Great Britain."

"What's going on there that's of interest to AXE?" Carter asked.

"Not only of interest to AXE and the United States," Hawk said, "but to every major power in the world."

"What?" Carter said. "This *is* just a small island we're talking about, isn't it?"

"A small country," Hawk corrected, "but then so is Kuwait, and look at the power it and the Arab Emirates hold."

"Yes, sir, but they've got oil—" Carter began, and then he realized what he said. "Don't tell me that Santa Caribe has discovered oil?"

"No," Hawk said. "Not oil."

"Then what?"

Hawk hesitated a moment, then said, "Cardium."

"That's used for nuclear reactor rods, isn't it?" Carter asked.

"Among other things, yes," Hawk said. "It was actually not essential that you know that."

"Great," Carter growled, a little annoyed at the AXE chief's secretive manner. "I suppose the leader

6

of this new country is being inundated with offers from all over the world for the cardium they've found, right?''

"Indeed, and from many Third World nations as well,'' Hawk said.

"And who has the inside track?''

"Actually, the United States just about had a deal wrapped up,'' Hawk explained.

"And?''

"And President Bili Makumbo was assassinated before the deal could be, ah, consummated.''

"Which puts us, and the rest of the world, back at square one,'' Carter finished.

"Unless we can do something about it.''

"Do you want me to go and make a personal plea to the new president of Santa Caribe on behalf of the United States?''

"That would be a little difficult,'' Hawk said, "since Santa Caribe has no formal leader at the present time. The country is in a state of utter chaos, with two separate factions fighting for power.''

"By fighting do you mean—''

"By fighting I mean revolution, civil war, whatever you want to call it.''

"I assume there's one side we're hoping will win, correct? And we'll help that group a bit?''

"Exactly, N3,'' Hawk said. "We've got to take a hand in this mess and make sure the right side wins.''

"The side Makumbo was on?''

"Right. If the other side wins, Santa Caribe is most likely to do its trading with Russia.''

"Or China?''

"Just as bad," Hawk said.

"So you do want me to go to Santa Caribe—"

"In an advisory capacity . . . unofficially. Lend your assistance to Makumbo's supporters and make sure they come out the winners."

"Yes, sir," Carter said, starting to get up. "When do I leave?"

"It's not going to be easy," Hawk cautioned him. "If I thought it would be, I'd be sending someone else."

"I understand," Carter said. "How do I get there?"

"Surreptitiously," Hawk said. "There is a single-airstrip airport there, but it has been closed down since the assassination, as have all the ports."

"No one is allowed in?"

"Or out."

"Do we have people there?"

"There are a few American tourists who have been unlucky enough to be caught up in this, yes," Hawk said, "but if you mean does AXE have anyone there, the answer is yes, but we don't know how much good she'll do you."

"She?"

Hawk turned a page in the file and said, "Her name is Megan Ward. She works in central filing. Do you know her?"

"Can't say that I do," Carter replied.

"That's surprising," Hawk said slyly. "I would have thought you knew virtually every female member of this organization."

"Sorry to disappoint you," Carter said. "What is she doing there, anyway?"

"She was on vacation when Makumbo was killed," Hawk answered. "Here is her picture."

When Hawk passed it over, Carter was also surprised that he didn't know her. She was a lovely brunette, and he wondered how she had managed to escape his notice.

"She's lovely," he commented.

"That may be so," Hawk said, "but that won't help either one of you on Santa Caribe."

"You never know," Carter said. He had put a woman's beauty to good use on more than one occasion.

"In any case, you'll be flying to Florida, and from there you'll go by boat."

"To Santa Caribe?"

"About five miles out," Hawk corrected.

"Five miles out?" Carter asked. "And how do I get to Santa Caribe from there?"

Deadpan, Hawk looked at him. "You swim."

Before leaving Hawk's office, Carter was given the name of the man who would be his contact within the Makumbo faction on Santa Caribe.

"What about the vice-president and the rest of the cabinet members?" Carter asked. "Couldn't they hold the government together?"

"What cabinet?" Hawk said. "As for the vice-president, he was supposed to have been in the presidential limo, but when they found Makumbo's body, it was alone in the car."

"No bodyguard?"

"Makumbo's bodyguard's name was George Mahbee, and we think that he's the one who killed President Makumbo. Apparently he thought a takeover

9

would be easy once the president was out of the way.

"He was wrong."

"He underestimated the feeling that the people of Santa Caribe had for their leader."

"So now he's in a fight for control," Carter said. "But with whom? The vice-president?"

"Jules Berbick," Hawk explained, "still hasn't turned up. For all we know he's either dead or in hiding somewhere."

"Then who's Mahbee battling with?"

"You'll find that out when you get there. We haven't been able to find out just who is in command of the Makumbo supporters."

So Carter had to find out who that man was, and then do everything he could to put that man into power.

TWO

Carter could feel himself sweating inside his wet suit. The shark, apparently unable to make up its mind about this odd, shiny black fish, was circling while Carter continued his forward motion, swimming toward Santa Caribe. He guessed that the shark could follow him the whole way without approaching him, but he wasn't counting on it.

He remembered the last thing Hawk had told him before he left his office: it was entirely possible that the Russians were sending in someone of their own to help George Mahbee's side, and Carter idly wondered if the shark had been sent by Moscow.

Carter had a speargun and was fairly proficient with it, but he was not about to risk a shot at the shark while it was not posing an immediate threat to him. If he missed and angered the beast, or wounded it, it would be all over. He couldn't hope to outswim or outmaneuver it on its own turf. So he continued swimming, holding the gun at the ready, just in case.

The pack strapped to Carter's back seemed to gradually increase in weight, and he began to wonder if the island he was swimming toward wasn't somehow moving away from him.

The thirty-five-foot cruiser had dropped Carter into Santa Caribe's water exactly five miles from shore. He'd planned on a leisurely swim, pacing himself so his powerful crawl would cover the most distance with a minimum of fatigue. And it would have been a pleasant, if long, swim if it hadn't been for the fifteen-foot shark that didn't seem to be sure if he wanted a traveling companion or lunch.

Every so often the shark seemed to blend into the azure depths of the water, and Carter was unable to locate his escort. He simply had to hope that during one of those periods the shark wouldn't take it into his tiny little mind to charge him.

Fat chance.

Moments later the shark suddenly came into view again through the murky water, and it was swimming much more quickly than before. Carter barely had time to move as the shark charged him and went by, striking him with its dorsal fin. The blow on his arm caused him to drop the speargun, and now Carter was sweating even more.

His left arm was numb from the blow, and he reached for the knife on his belt with his right, keeping his eyes open for the shark. He considered the strong possibility that this assignment might end before it even got started.

Holding the knife tightly, Carter began to kick his legs faster. He forced himself to use his left arm, and gradually the feeling came back into it. He felt he was moving at a good pace when the shark raced by him from behind at top speed, making Carter feel as if he were standing still. He watched as the creature pulled ahead, then turned and seemed to study him. Suddenly it rocketed toward him, and Carter held out his knife. He wasn't at all sure where he could drive the knife to do the most damage, but he imagined that the shark's belly would be a good spot. As it approached, Carter abruptly stopped moving his arms and legs, which caused him to sink like a stone. When the shark passed directly above him, he drove the knife up and into the soft underbelly, and held onto it tightly, the blade forward. As he hoped, the shark's own momentum caused the knife to tear open its belly, almost yanking the blade from his grasp.

Without waiting to examine the damage he had done, he once again began to swim toward shore, his adrenaline adding new vigor to his strokes.

Finally, when he stood in waist-deep water, he went to replace the knife in his belt and noticed that the blade had broken off, probably still in the belly of the shark.

" 'Bye, Bruce," he said, discarding the hilt, and then he waded ashore and shed the wet suit, burying it high enough on the beach so it wouldn't be uncovered at high tide.

From the pack he took a nylon windbreaker, jeans, sneakers, and his weapons, all of which had been sealed in waterproof plastic bags. He took the time to affix Pierre to his inner thigh, and then he donned both

Wilhelmina and Hugo. Feeling fully dressed at last, he vacated the beach in favor of some high brush, and settled down to wait for his contact to come and get him.

Carter fell asleep, but even then he was never fully relaxed, and it was a very slight sound—a footstep causing a twig to snap—that awakened him, alert and ready. With Wilhelmina in hand he peered through his patch of brush and spotted a girl who seemed to be looking for something . . . or someone. She was not wearing any sort of a uniform, just tattered, dirty work clothes in which she probably fought and slept.

He waited until she was reasonably close to his hiding place, but not so close that he would startle her when he stepped out. She was armed, and he had no desire to be shot by mistake before he even got off the beach.

"Hello," Carter called out softly, and the girl stopped and turned quickly, a startled look on her face.

His first good, clear look at her told him that she wasn't really a girl, but a young woman, probably in her early twenties. She had long dark hair, parted in the center, and her frightened eyes were large and brown, set wide over a perfect nose. Her full-lipped mouth was slightly open, as if she were going to cry out. He found her face very appealing and was looking forward to seeing it wear expressions other than the surprised one she now wore.

"I hope you're looking for me," he went on, utilizing the opening phrase of the recognition code.

Her face relaxed as she examined him for a moment, and then she replied, "For hours on end."

Carter stepped away from his hiding place and returned Wilhelmina to his shoulder holster.

"Nick Carter," he said, introducing himself.

"My name is Liza," she said. "I'm here to guide you."

Her skin was a deep golden brown, and he wondered if that was its natural shade or a result of the strong, tropical sun.

"You know why I'm here, then."

"To help, they said," she answered. Then she added, "To help yourself, that's what I think."

"Is that so?" he asked.

"Your country wouldn't have sent you here if we didn't have something it wanted."

"And what's that?"

"Damned if I know," she replied candidly. She obviously had no idea what it was her little country had that made it so interesting to the big boys.

That made them even, of course.

"You're looking a gift horse in the mouth, aren't you?" Carter said.

"What?" she asked, looking puzzled. Her "puzzled" was just as fetching as her "startled" had been.

"Does it matter why I'm here to help, as long as I help?"

"That remains to be seen," she answered dubiously. "We'd better get going. Mahbee's men sometimes check the beaches."

Carter ducked back to his hiding place to pick up his pack, then quickly returned and said, "Lead on, Liza."

● ● ●

During their trip, Liza brought Nick Carter as up-to-date on her country's affairs as she could. George Mahbee was in command of most of President Makumbo's soldiers, to whom he had apparently made big promises. A small number of the late president's army had fled to the hills and had joined in the fight against Mahbee.

"Are they trained soldiers?" Carter asked.

"Mahbee's men are better trained than we are," Liza said. "Many of the ones who stayed were foreign mercenaries, working for pay. Mahbee has offered them more than they were getting from President Makumbo."

"And the ones who left?"

"They are countrymen—farmers and fishermen. What training they received they got from the mercenaries."

Not good, Carter thought. Even if there were a comparable number of them, they would be no match for experienced mercenaries, no matter how much training they had received while in Makumbo's service.

"Did they bring their weapons with them?"

"Yes," she said, "and some extra weapons they stole from the armory."

At least the weapons were comparable, but it was the experience and ability behind those weapons that made them deadly.

"Does Mahbee's army have any heavy artillery?"

"Not very much," she said. "No tanks or anything like that, if that's what you mean."

"Flamethrowers, bazookas, anything like that?"

Liza shrugged her shoulders. "I don't know. You'll have to ask Willem."

"Willem?"

"He knows much more than I do," she said. "All they do is send me with messages and make me act as a guide . . . like now." The young woman's tone was bitter.

"You want to fight, eh?"

"Yes!" she replied with feeling. "I want to get our country back for the people. George Mahbee wants to use Santa Caribe to make himself rich."

"Maybe you'll get your chance to fight, Liza," he told her.

"I hope so."

She was wearing a Luger on her hip that had seen better days, and Carter hoped that the rest of the armaments were in better condition than that particular piece. Since she had not seen any fighting yet, the men in charge had probably simply not seen fit to give her a first-class weapon—if, indeed, they had any.

"Is Willem the guy in charge?" Carter asked.

"He calls himself a general," she said. "He's not, but he is in charge—as much as anybody is."

"Is he the man you're fighting to put into power in President Makumbo's place?"

She snorted. "Oh, no!"

"Who is, then?"

Again Liza shrugged. "I don't know that. Only Willem and a handful of others do. They are afraid that someone will try and kill him before we even get him into power."

"That's a valid worry," Carter admitted, but one of

the first things he wanted to establish was who he was fighting for.

"Are we going to the city?" Carter asked after they'd walked a few miles.

"No," she said. "I'm taking you to one of our camps. You'll be taken to Caribe City later."

Hawk had told Carter that he would be moved into one of the capital's hotels, into a room that had been taken by a tall, dark-haired American who took all his meals from room service and never left. This would make it easy for Carter to move into the room, a reclusive tourist who had already been on the island when "Mahbee's Law" had been declared.

"By you?" he asked.

"Probably," she replied, not sounding happy about it.

Carter had been walking behind her most of the way, and even though the clothing she was wearing had been meant for a larger person, he sensed that she had a good body, an athletic body. It showed in the way she walked and in the fact that she was not breathing hard despite the heat and the distance they had traveled.

"I don't know about you," Carter said, "but I'm ready for a rest. I had a bit of a swim this morning, remember?"

She turned and planted her hands on her hips, staring down her nose at him as he bent over to put his pack on the ground.

"What's in there?" she asked.

"Just some things I thought might be handy to have along," he said, sitting on a large rock. "You can sit

18

and rest too," he told her. "I won't tell anyone."

She gave him a superior look but finally planted her shapely bottom on a flat rock. She was perspiring, and it glistened in the hollow of her throat, but she was not breathing hard.

"What do they think one man can do?" she asked suddenly, as if the question had been preying on her mind for some time.

"I don't know," Carter admitted, "but there was some talk about Mahbee bringing in someone also."

"Russian?"

"Maybe."

"Mahbee will let them in and they will take us over," she said in disgust. "We did not have independence for very long, but a taste was all we needed to know that we want to keep it."

"Well, I may only be one man, Liza, but I'll do what I can to help you keep it."

She regarded him for a moment, then gave him a tiny smile. "As you said, I shouldn't look a gift horse in the mouth."

"Excuse me for saying so," Carter said, "but I don't detect any kind of an accent. You are from Santa Caribe, aren't you?"

"I was born here, but I was educated in the United States. When we obtained our independence and President Makumbo was elected, I came back here to live."

"And now to fight."

She sniffed and made a face. "Some soldier," she muttered.

"We all contribute in different ways—"

"Don't give me that baloney!" she exploded, cutting him off. "I've been getting enough of that patronizing garbage lately. Do you know what I think it is?"

"No, what?"

"I don't think they feel that I belong."

"Because you lived in the States for so long, you mean?"

"Right. You know," she said, slapping her hands on her knees and standing up, "I don't even know why I care. I've got a master's degree, I could have had a good job if I'd stayed . . ."

"They why did you come back?"

"I'll bet you think I'm some sort of a patriotic saint, huh?" she asked. "That I gave it all up to come back and live in my native land." She put her hand over her heart, a movement that matched the overly dramatic tone of her voice.

"That's not it?"

She dropped her hand. "Yes, that's part of it. The other part is that, master's and all, I couldn't find a job. What do you think of that?"

"We've a troubled economy," he said.

"Good," she said. "You didn't patronize me. We might get along after all, Mr. Carter."

"Nick," he said, "and that's what I've been trying to do since we met."

"Yeah," she said, "I know. I'm sorry . . . Nick. I'm getting a little crazy, that's all. I want to help, and they won't let me."

"Well, Liza," Carter said, standing up and shrugging his way into his pack, "I know I'm going to need help while I'm here, and lots of it. Do you think we could get your leader—Willem—to let you help me?''

''Could we?'' she asked like a small child. ''You bet we could, Nick! He'll be only too happy to get me off his back.''

And just like that, Nick Carter and Liza became the best of friends.

THREE

"I hear something," Carter said after they had walked a short distance, and they both stopped to listen.

"I hear it, too. It sounds like a motor."

They had come to the road only moments before, and now Carter said, "We'd better get off the road . . . unless your people are sending a car to pick us up."

"Ha," Liza said. "What car?"

"Then let's move," he hissed, and they sprinted off the road and into hiding just as a jeep rounded the corner.

"Mahbee's soldiers," she whispered.

He nodded, and they watched as the jeep with four uniformed soldiers passed very close, then kept on going. The men in the jeep seemed unconcerned with the possibility that there might be someone hiding off the side of the road.

"They don't look like they're looking for anyone

in particular,'' Carter commented after the jeep had passed them.

''They're probably on their way to the beach,'' she said as they both stood up and brushed themselves off. ''Still, I suppose we'd better avoid the roads from now on. It'll mean a longer walk,'' she said apologetically, ''and not over flat land, either.''

''I can take it if you can,'' he said, ''only I didn't think this island was this big.''

''It's a lot bigger on foot than it is by car,'' she told him. ''Let's go.''

By the time they finally reached their destination, even Liza was breathing hard from the constant uphill walking.

''This is it,'' Liza announced suddenly, and Carter looked around in surprise. All he saw was a small, one-room house, although ''hut'' would have been a better description.

''Where are we?'' he asked. ''This couldn't be your headquarters . . .''

''This is where they asked me to bring you,'' she said. ''Let's see if anyone is here.''

They approached the hut warily, and Carter moved ahead of Liza so that he could go in first with Wilhelmina in hand.

''Empty,'' he announced as he examined the room while crouched down in the doorway on one knee. He stood up inside and stepped aside to allow Liza to enter, then closed the door behind them and put away his gun.

''I guess we'll just have to wait,'' she said. ''I

wonder if there's anything to eat here.''

While she searched the room for something edible, Carter looked out the window, back the way they had come, to see if anyone had been following them.

"Anything?" she asked.

"No," he answered, "nothing. What about you?" he added, turning away from the window. "Anything to eat?"

"Not even any coffee," she said glumly. "I guess we'll just have to sit and wait."

"You didn't find a deck of cards, did you?" he asked.

"Sorry."

"When are they supposed to be here?"

"Well," she said, looking at her watch, "to tell the truth, we were supposed to have been here a half hour ago. Staying off the roads cost us time."

"You mean they might have been here and gone?"

"With Mahbee's soldiers around, it isn't healthy to stay in one place for too long, Nick, but I wouldn't worry. If they did leave, they'll probably come back later."

"And what do we do in the meantime?" he asked.

She noticed him looking at her, smiled, and said, "Just don't get any ideas, friend. I don't do it on the first date."

They talked awhile, and Carter found himself sympathizing with Liza's plight. It was obvious that she was a very intelligent woman, and he was sorry that she had not been able to establish herself in a career in the

United States. Most of all, however, he sympathized with her as far as wanting to fight for her young country and not being allowed to contribute the way she would have liked.

"If Willem agrees to assign me to you, maybe that will all change," she said hopefully.

"We'll have to wait and see," Carter said, glancing out the window for the umpteenth time.

"Maybe we can—" she started to say, but he cut her off with a wave of his hand.

"Somebody's coming," he said quickly.

She rose from the table and hurried to the window. Pressing up against him, she peered outside to see if she could identify whoever was approaching.

"They're on foot," she said, "but I can't make them out yet. They're too far away."

"No problem," he assured her. "They're getting closer by the minute."

They both stood by the window, anxiously waiting for the group of men to come close enough to be identified. Carter was very aware of Liza's hip pressed against his thigh and of the heat emanating from her body. He was also able to tell that she did indeed have a fine, full figure beneath the shapeless clothing she was wearing. If she was as aware of him, she did not show it.

"Anything yet?" he asked.

Holding her breath, she shook her head and continued to stare out the window. He could feel the tension in her body and imagined that he could also feel her heart beating faster than it did normally. Then, suddenly, the tension drained from her body as if floodgates had been opened, and he knew that she had recognized someone.

"That's Willem in the front," she said. "It's all right."

Five men approached the shack at a fast trot now, looking around them to make sure they had not been spotted.

Liza moved away from the window and hurried to the door to greet them.

"Willem," she breathed, backing away to allow the leader to enter.

"Liza," the man said, clasping a firm hand on her shoulder. It was not, Carter thought, a casual gesture, but one of genuine affection.

"This is Nick Carter, the man from America," she said, indicating Carter who was still by the window.

"You were late," Willem said, turning to face him.

"We ran across some of Mahbee's men in a jeep," Carter explained.

"We thought it better to stay off the roads after that," Liza chimed in.

"We've been here too long, then," Willem said. "We will go somewhere else, and then we can talk. Come."

He took hold of Liza's elbow possessively and propelled her toward the door. She threw Carter a glance of helplessness over her shoulder, and he picked up his pack and followed them out. The other four men had remained outside as lookouts, and now they all fell in line behind Willem and Liza, with Carter bringing up the rear.

Willem was a big man, dark-skinned like Liza, and

Carter had the distinct impression that the man was not happy that he was there. That would make things harder, because it was always difficult to help someone who didn't want your help, but Carter's job was to try, and that's what he intended to do.

Carter stayed at the rear of the small procession, and every so often he noticed Liza looking back at him. Once, while she was looking at him, Willem spoke to her sharply and she turned her head around quickly, but she continued to steal glances at Carter from time to time.

Willem was young, probably not yet thirty, and he took his leadership very seriously. This would pose another problem, because the man would be sure to look upon Carter as competition. Carter was going to have to try and make it clear from the start that he was not there to lead, but to assist.

As Carter was starting to wonder how much further they had to go, they stopped abruptly. He continued on until he was standing next to Willem and Liza.

"What's wrong?" he asked.

"Nothing," Willem said. When he did not offer an explanation as to why they had stopped, Liza said, "We're here, Nick."

"Where?" he asked, looking around.

She pointed ahead of them to where there was a steep hill and said, "There's a man-made cavern carved into that hillside. You can't see it from here, can you?"

"No."

"That's why it's an ideal place for us to have our headquarters," she said rather proudly.

"Let's go," Willem snapped. "We will talk inside."

Carter followed them to the hillside, and when they reached it, two of the other men moved in to clear away some cleverly arranged loose brush, and Carter saw the entrance.

"Very ingenious," he admitted.

"Yes," Willem said, and he led the way into the cavern.

The walls and ceiling were of earth and rock, but in certain places they were reinforced by wood beams. Provisions were stacked on one side, and among them Carter could see some weapons and explosives, but he did not comment on them. He did not want to start off his association with Willem by criticizing the man. Later, when they were on firmer footing with each other, he would suggest that the weapons and explosives be kept elsewhere.

There was a long wooden table with benches in the center of the cavern, and Willem walked to it and set his weapon, an M-16, down on a bench.

"Liza," he called, "would you and Mr. Carter come over here, please?" The man had said only four words to Carter thus far—"You were late" and then later, "Nothing"—and he did not yet seem inclined to open up.

Carter and Liza approached the table and sat down. The other four men in the party sat on the floor elsewhere in the cavern, smoking and relaxing.

"I think it's only fair to tell you, Carter," Willem said, "that I did not want you here."

"Fair enough," Carter said, "and I think I can understand why. We're both going to have to make the best of the situation."

"Agreed," Willem replied, "but there is something else we must both agree on."

"What's that?"

"I am the leader here."

"I won't argue with that," Carter said. "I'm only here to assist your cause—"

"To further your country's cause," Willem broke in.

"Correct," Carter said, "but either we both win, or we both lose; there's no two ways about it."

"You're right," Willem said in a low voice, but he still did not look very happy.

"Now let me ask you something," Carter said.

"What?"

"You are the leader. Does that mean that when your cause is won you'll be in the president's seat?"

"No," Willem said. "I am privileged to serve our next president as his general."

"And who will that be?" Carter asked.

"That is not necessary for you to know," Willem said angrily. "You are here to help us no matter who our next president will be, isn't that so?"

"That's true enough," Carter said, "But I would still like to know who the man is. If you don't have the authority to tell me, perhaps you can ask him for permission."

Willem stiffened and said, "I will ask him."

"Good. Can we get to the briefing now? I want to get into the city as soon as possible."

"We will get you to your nice comfortable hotel, Mr. Carter, have no fear," Willem said with a sneer in his voice.

Willem quickly ran down the situation for Carter. Mahbee had established himself and his forces in the capital, and was depending on his former position as Makumbo's bodyguard to aid him in becoming the next president. The opposition—the man Willem and his people were fighting for—was in hiding, and would come out if and when his forces were triumphant, or if he were elected to the presidency.

"When is the election?" Carter asked.

"A date has not yet been set," Willem said. "Mahbee is stalling, hoping that his people will be able to defeat us—or find the only man capable of defeating him in the election and killing him."

"Do you have any representatives in the city?"

"We have some undercover people there," Willem said, "but if they were discovered by Mahbee, they'd be killed."

"Mahbee seems to have just about everything but the official position," Carter said.

"That he does," Willem said, "but while we live, he will never get that."

"Well, if we can see about getting me into the city, I'll see what I can do to help."

"What can you do?" Willem asked.

"I won't know that for a while, Willem," Carter said. "I've got to look over the situation myself before I can make a suggestion as to what I can do to help."

"I see," Willem said, obviously unimpressed. "If

you will give us some time to rest, I will have someone take you into the city.''

Carter was about to ask specifically that Liza be that person, but just at that moment she caught his eye and shook her head slightly. Carter swallowed his words, guessing that she wanted to approach Willem herself about the matter.

"All right," Carter said. "I can use a rest myself."

While Carter was waiting for Willem to decide who should guide him into the city, he walked over to where the weapons were stacked and examined them briefly. He saw that the arsenal was an international assortment containing American, Russian, Czech, and even some Israeli weapons. The predominant gun seemed to be the American-made M-16, and Carter wondered if Santa Caribe had gotten them directly from the Pentagon or from a munitions dealer.

Against another wall of the cavern were piled some canned and dried rations.

Carter turned and caught Willem and Liza involved in a very animated conversation, the subject of which was not hard to guess. At one point Willem reached out to grasp her elbow, and she shook him off violently. From that point on they talked without touching and eventually separated, both looking tense. Willem went to talk to his men, and Liza walked over to Carter.

"What's the verdict?"

"Willem has agreed to let me take you to the city," she said. She was obviously still upset from the conversation.

"Reluctantly, I gather."

"He said that it was too dangerous for me to go there," she said, "but that's not the real reason.

"Are the two of you, uh, very close?"

She looked at Carter, raised her chin, and said, "We were in the past, but he has no right to deny me my right to help for that reason. There is nothing between us now but friendship and comradeship."

"I see."

Carter was about to say something else, but he broke off when he saw Willem approaching them.

"Liza will take you to the edge of the city," he told Carter while staring daggers at the young woman. "Someone will meet you there and smuggle you to your hotel where you will switch places with the man who is now in your room."

"How do I get in touch with you?" Carter asked.

"The man who takes you into the hotel will be your contact with us."

"Okay. There's one other thing."

"Yes?"

"I want to get in touch with a woman named Megan Ward, an American tourist."

"A friend of yours?" Liza asked.

"Probably more than a friend," Willem said pointedly. "What is she doing here?"

"She was on vacation," Carter said, "and just happened to be in Santa Caribe when Makumbo was killed."

"Is she one of your people?"

"Not really, but since she's here, we'd like to try and use her to our advantage."

Willem nodded and said, "We will locate her for

you. It is possible that she will be staying in the same hotel with you. It is a popular one with tourists.''

"That would make it easier," Carter said.

"We will let you know," Willem said. He turned to Liza and said, "You can start whenever you're ready . . . and be careful."

"I'm always careful, Willem," she told him.

"Mr. Carter," the man went on, ignoring her remark, "I hope that you will be of some assistance to us."

"So do I."

"I look forward to hearing from you," Willem said, and then added, "soon."

The man called Willem was in the presence of the man he was fighting to put into President Makumbo's seat.

"The man from the United States has arrived?" the man asked. He was lying in a small wood-framed bed, and there was a swathe of bandages encircling his upper torso. In one or two spots the blood could be seen seeping through the gauze, but the man's wounds had actually been bound and treated very effectively. There was an excellent chance that he would actually live to serve if he were elected.

"He has," Willem said, tight-lipped.

"Ah, and you do not approve."

"We do not need him."

"Of course we do, Willem," the man replied, using the man's assigned name. "In fact, even he might not be able to help us defeat the treachery of George Mahbee."

34

"We will defeat Mahbee," Willem said, "and you will be the next president of Santa Caribe."

"That is what we all hope for," the man said. He was about to say more when he suddenly began coughing, and Willem hurried to pour his leader a glass of water and hand it to him.

The man drank some of the water in small sips, and when the coughing subsided he said, "Thank you," and handed the glass back to Willem.

"Are you all right?"

"I'm fine," the man replied, waving a hand weakly, "I just need some more rest."

"I will leave you," Willem said, turning toward the door.

"Willem, before you leave . . ."

"Yes?"

"Trust the American," the man on the bed said. "He is our only chance to defeat Mahbee. Our only chance."

"Yes . . ." Willem said, but as he left he still had his doubts about Nick Carter. He did not like the way he and Liza had been looking at each other, and the way Liza insisted on being able to work with the man.

But, of course, that had no bearing on his inability to trust the man or on the fact that he disliked him.

No bearing at all.

FOUR

Liza guided Carter to the outskirts of the capital, Caribe City. She was oddly silent during the entire trip, and Carter was not exactly sure to what he could attribute that, but he respected her mood and did not try to engage her in conversation.

"This is as far as I go," she said when they reached their destination.

"This is where you hand me over to someone else?" he asked.

"I'll wait with you," she said. "Willem also agreed that if and when you send word that you want to talk to someone, it will be me that you'll see."

"That suits me," Carter said. "I don't think your Willem and I will ever be great friends."

"He's not my Willem."

"Sorry."

"No," she said, "I'm sorry. I shouldn't take it out on you. Lately whenever I talk to Willem, we both end up arguing. You were right before; we used to be 'very close,' but that's over.''

"Does he know that?"

"He refuses to believe it, but that doesn't change anything.''

"Well, I hope everything works out for you.''

"I hope it works out for my country first,'' she said. "I'll worry about myself later.''

"That's an admirable attitude, Liza,'' Carter said, "and I'm not patronizing you.''

"No, I know you're not,'' she said, "and I appreciate it, Nick.''

At that point they both heard someone coming and shrank into the brush.

"It's all right,'' Liza said, "it's Ollie.''

"Ollie?''

"He will take you to the Hotel Caribe,'' she said, standing up. "He works there as a bellboy.''

"Well, that'll be handy,'' Carter said.

They both stepped from the brush together to meet Ollie, who turned out to be a boy in his late teens, tall and thin.

"Here, Ollie,'' Liza said, waving to him.

"Liza, hello,'' he said, coming over and touching her arm. The look on his face told Carter that here was another man fighting for the cause who was probably in love with the dark-haired young woman.

"Ollie, this is Nick Carter.''

"No, it's not,'' Ollie said.

"What do you mean?'' Liza asked.

Carter spoke before the young man could.

"I think what Ollie means is that I'm not registered at the hotel by that name."

"That's right," Ollie said, looking disappointed that Carter had caught on as quickly as he did.

"Happy to meet you, Ollie," Carter said, putting out his hand.

Ollie was a handsome black youth, his dark skin accentuating a set of very white teeth that seemed to sparkle when the boy smiled, as he did while shaking Carter's hand.

"A pleasure to meet you, sir. I have long wanted to meet a member of the American CIA."

"Who told you I was with the CIA?" Carter asked.

"I merely assumed . . ." Ollie began, then trailed off. "You aren't with the CIA?"

"I'm sorry, Ollie. No, I'm not."

The boy looked disappointed again for a moment, then brightened and smiled. "Oh, well, then I still have something to look forward to, don't I?"

Carter laughed and said, "I guess you do."

"Ollie, take Nick to the hotel now, and be careful that no one sees him entering," Liza said.

"I will be very careful, don't worry," he told her. "Will you be staying in the city, Liza?"

"No, but you can get in touch with me if Nick needs anything, and I'll come."

Ollie looked glum again, but he did not seem to stay that way for very long.

"Okay, Liza," he said. "And you be careful going back."

"I will, Ollie," she said, then turned to Carter.

"I'm glad you're here, Nick. I think that maybe we need even more help than you can give, but I'm glad you're here."

"Thanks," Carter said. "After a couple of days I should have some idea of what, if anything, I can do, and then I'll have Ollie send for you and we'll talk."

"I'll be waiting," she said. Impulsively she leaned forward and kissed Carter swiftly on the cheek. "Good luck, Nick."

"You take care, Liza," he said, and then she was through the brush and gone.

Carter stared after her for a moment, then turned to Ollie and said, "Okay, Ollie, I'm ready when you are."

"I'm always ready, Mr. Carter," Ollie said.

"You'd better call me Nick, Ollie," he said. "When we leave this spot, 'Mr. Carter' will be staying behind."

"Okay, Nick. Follow me."

It was dark as Ollie led Carter through the streets of Caribe City, and from time to time Ollie would pull him into a darkened doorway as a soldier or two approached.

"Curfew," Ollie explained the first time, and after that, Carter simply followed the boy whenever he melted into the shadows to avoid notice by a soldier.

Before long they were on the grounds of the hotel, and Ollie picked his way through trees and shrubs until they were at the back door.

"I have a key," Ollie said, smiling so that his teeth shone brightly in the dark, lit by the moon.

"Ollie, you're a wonder," Carter said, and the boy's smile increased in width and wattage.

Ollie approached the door, slid the key into the lock, and when he had it opened, signaled Carter to follow. When Carter entered, the boy closed and locked the door behind them, then led Carter down a narrow corridor to a stairway.

"I hope you don't mind walking up to the fourth floor," Ollie said in a low voice.

"After the traveling I did today through your country," Carter replied, "a four-story climb will be like a vacation."

"We do have a lot of hills, don't we?" Ollie asked with a chuckle, and then he led the way up the stairs.

He reached the fourth-floor landing half a flight ahead of Carter and was waiting with a wide smile when the AXE agent caught up to him.

"You're in good shape, aren't you?" Carter asked when he reached the landing and was standing next to the young islander.

"Excellent shape, sir," Ollie said proudly. "Your room is just down the hall."

"What about the man who has been staying in it?"

"We moved him out today," Ollie said. "The room has been vacant since this morning."

"What about the maids?"

"I took care of the maids, Nick," Ollie said. "Have no fear; no one will be able to tell that you have not been the man in the room for the past week."

"You're very efficient," Carter said, complimenting the boy again because he knew Ollie thrived on it.

"Thank you, sir," Ollie said. "Wait and I will check the hallway."

Carter waited while Ollie went through the door to check it out. A minute later the bellboy came back and said, "The coast is clear. Follow me—quickly."

Carter followed Ollie through the door and down the hall, and when they were outside the room Ollie turned, smiled, and said, "I have the key."

"Wonderful."

Ollie opened the door, allowed Carter to go in first, looked up and down the hallway, and then followed him inside, shutting the door behind them.

"I enjoy this cape and dagger stuff," he told Carter.

"Cloak," Carter corrected him.

"Cape and cloak?" Ollie asked, looking puzzled.

"Never mind, Ollie," Carter said. "Just don't enjoy yourself so much that you get careless."

"I would never do that," Ollie assured him. "This is very serious business."

"Yes, it is," Carter agreed.

"Would you like me to show you around the room?"

"That's all right, Ollie. I'll show myself around. Right now I think I'd just like to take a shower and unwind."

"Would you like me to send up some spirits?"

"Uh, spirits," Carter said. "Yeah, okay, that sounds like a good idea."

"I get lots of good ideas, Nick," Ollie said. "I could also send you a woman, if you like."

"Send me a bottle of bourbon," Carter said, "and let's leave it at that for now."

"Very good, sir," Ollie said, and for a moment Carter thought the boy was going to salute.

"There is one other thing you can do for me," Carter said.

"Anything."

"Find out if there is a woman named Megan Ward registered at this hotel."

"Megan Ward?" Ollie asked. "Is this lady a friend of yours?'

"Let's say she's someone I'm very anxious to meet," Carter said.

"Is she pretty?"

"Very."

"I will find out for you," Ollie said with a wink.

"Discreetly," Carter added. With all of the energy that Ollie seemed to possess, Carter hoped the boy had enough self-control not to be too obvious.

"But of course, sir," Ollie said. "That is the way I always work."

After Ollie left, Carter took a quick, hot shower and was out in time to accept his bottle of bourbon at the door from another bellhop. He watched the man's face closely to see if he would recognize the fact that there was a different man in the room now, but the bored look on the man's face never changed, not even when Carter tipped him heavily.

Carter went into the bathroom to get a glass, then poured himself a drink and carried it to the closet with him. Hawk had told him that the clothing in the hotel room would be his size. Checking now, he found a complete wardrobe in the closet and bureau, so he selected something casual and dressed, then went into the living room of the two-room suite.

He sat on the couch with his drink, looked at his watch, and was surprised to find that it was still fairly early in the evening. The swim and all the walking he had done that day had tired him out, and he had felt that it was much later. It was only nine o'clock, and he decided not to stay in his room. He thought he might as well go down to the bar right away and find out if anyone would notice that he was not the same man who had originally checked into the hotel.

In the elevator he reminded himself that he was now Nick Taylor so that he would respond to that name if someone called out to him.

Nick Taylor entered the hotel bar and ordered a bourbon on the rocks. He looked around, giving anyone who cared to notice a clear look at his face.

When the bartender returned with the drink, Carter said, "Could you start a tab, please?"

"Of course, sir."

"My name is Nick Taylor, and I'm in room four-oh-five."

"Very good, Mr. Taylor," the bartender said and did not otherwise react to Carter's claim that he was Taylor.

Carter sipped his drink and looked over the room again. Almost all the guests were young, obviously on vacation, and, didn't look terribly put out by the fact that "Mahbee's Law"—as opposed to martial law—had extended their stay. Indeed, most of them were probably happy to have an excuse not to go back home, and back to work.

Carter called the bartender over and asked, "How dangerous would it be for me to go for a walk?"

"If you stay on the hotel grounds or on our beach, you should have no problem at all, sir," the bartender said, "but I would not advise walking on the city streets. The soldiers would not be very gentle with you if they caught you."

"I see."

"This is the first time I've seen you in the bar, Mr. Taylor," the man observed.

"Yes," Carter replied. "A vacation is a hell of a time to come down with some kind of a bug. But considering what's happened here, being indoors last week wasn't such a bad idea."

"I suppose so, sir," the man said. "If you do go for a walk, please remember what I said."

"I will," Carter said. "Thanks."

Carter sat through another drink, then ordered a third and took it out on the veranda with him. He could see the beach from where he was, and the full moon had a twin floating in the water. The beach itself was empty, and he decided that he would go down there and take a walk by the water. It would be quite different from all of the other walking he had done during the day.

The bartender's remark had taken a load from his mind, and he felt that his "masquerade" would most probably go off without a hitch. Without that to worry about, he could devote his undivided attention to other things.

The first order of business come morning would be locating and talking to Megan Ward, and finding out just how much assistance she might be. Then he'd have to do some touristing and see if he could find out how much of a hold George Mahbee had on Santa Caribe.

In the meantime he'd have to keep his eyes open; Hawk was sure that the Russians were going to send in someone of their own to assist Mahbee, and with a little luck he'd be able to recognize his opposite number. By the same token, whoever it was might also be able to recognize him. However, if they knew each other, it would be that much easier to deal with the situation. He wouldn't have to be looking over his shoulder, wondering if one of the people behind him was sighting in on his back.

Walking on the beach soon wore thin. It wasn't an easy thing to do in shoes, and it would also have been easier to do with a woman beside him. He headed back to the hotel, hoping he'd be able to get a late dinner. He suddenly realized how hungry he was.

In the hotel dinning room, one of the waiters made a remark similar to the one the bartender had made, but he did not seem to find anything unusual about "Mr. Taylor."

Carter eavesdropped on a conversation going on at the next table between a young couple who had come to Santa Caribe on their honeymoon. They were wondering when, if ever, the restrictions on travel would be lifted so they could go back home and get on with their lives. Not until Mahbee was either defeated or officially in office, Carter thought.

The dinner was very good, and the wine was excellent. At least he wouldn't starve while he was being Nick Taylor on Santa Caribe, but Willem had a point when he asked what Carter thought he could do. He was, after all, only one man. The only way he would really be able to make a strong, valid contribution was if Willem and his people trusted him completely. The same would be true for Mahbee. If he was accepting assistance from the Russians, he would have to completely trust the man they sent.

If Carter and the Russian were given the trust they required, the struggle for power on Santa Caribe could very well turn into a chess game between the two of them. Unfortunately for Carter, the Russian would have one major advantage over him.

He'd know who his king was, and Carter wouldn't, and even in a game, it was important to know what you were fighting for.

FIVE

In the morning, Carter called room service and ordered breakfast, and he specified that he would like Ollie to bring it up.

"As you wish, sir," the operator said. It was not unusual for guests to request certain bellboys. To get what they wanted from a big hotel, guests would often have to cultivate certain employees.

After fifteen minutes there was a knock on the door, and when Carter opened it, Ollie stood there behind a breakfast cart, beaming his blinding smile.

"Room service," he announced through his grin.

"Bring it in, Ollie," Carter said. "I hope this is as good as the food served in the dining room."

"You ate in the dining room?" Ollie asked. "Wasn't that kind of dangerous?"

"Maybe," Carter said, inspecting the food on the cart, "but I had to find out right away if I was going to be accepted as Nick Taylor. I don't need any surprises later.''·

"I guess not," Ollie agreed. "You must know what you are doing, or the CIA wouldn't have sent you here."

"I told you last night that I'm not with the CIA."

"Oh, right," Ollie said with a nod, "you're not. I forgot. Whatever you say, Nick."

It was obvious that Ollie had thought it over and decided that Carter was with the CIA and had his own reasons for denying it. Carter was willing to play along and decided not to argue the point further.

"While I eat," Carter said, "why don't you tell me about Megan Ward?"

"She is registered at this hotel," Ollie said, "which is not unusual. This is the finest hotel on the island."

"The food is certainly good," Carter said around a mouthful of eggs.

"Everything here is the best," Ollie said proudly, as if he owned the hotel instead of just worked for it.

"Especially the personalized service, eh?"

"Right," Ollie said, beaming again.

"Megan Ward?"

"Oh, yes," Ollie said, searching his pockets. "I wrote down her room number."

Carter paid attention to his breakfast until Ollie finally found the right pocket.

"Here it is," the bellboy said, handing over a slip of paper.

"She's on this floor," he said, reading the number.

"That's right. Just down the hall. Some coincidence, isn't it?"

Carter didn't like coincidences, but he had to admit that this might actually be one.

"Yeah," he said. "Some coincidence."

"And she is very lovely, as you said," Ollie commented.

"Oh? And how do you know that?"

"I have delivered room service to her room too," he said. "She is not a very good tipper, but then I don't think she can afford to be."

"How can she afford to stay in this hotel'"

"I have made a study of hotel guests," Ollie said very seriously, "and she is one of those who has saved for a long time to take a vacation, and then does not have the money to really enjoy it."

"Aren't there women who save their money to go on a vacation and hope to find a man to enjoy it with who'll also pick up the tab?"

"The tab?" Ollie asked, frowning. "Oh, I see what you mean. Yes, I have seen women like that, but this is not one of them. I think Miss Ward is very shy, and perhaps sorry that she chose Santa Caribe for her vacation."

"Especially now."

"Yes, of course," Ollie said. "Before the assassination, she was sorry enough, but she's even more so now. I don't think she's left the hotel grounds since the trouble started."

"Is she afraid?"

"I believe so."

"I'll have to go to her room to see her, then," Carter said, putting down his fork. "This might work out for the best. As long as no one sees me going in, then no one will be able to put us together."

"A man and a woman getting together is not unusual at a Caribbean resort hotel," Ollie point out.

"I don't doubt it," Carter said, "but I'd rather not play it that way just now. I'll talk to her first and see what happens."

"Would you like me to take you over there?" Ollie asked eagerly.

"No, I think you've done enough for now, Ollie. I'll make my own introductions to the lady, thanks."

"Only trying to help."

"I know you are, and you've been a great help. I'll call on you again in the near future."

"I certainly hope so. I'm anxious to help the CIA help my country—oh, I'm sorry!" the teen-ager said, clapping a hand over his mouth. "You're not the CIA. I forgot."

"That's all right, Ollie," Carter said. "Just go back to work and don't worry about it."

"Yes, sir!"

"Dismissed, Ollie," Carter said, "dismissed."

The young man backed to the door and opened it, then hurried out, closing it behind him.

As eager as Ollie obviously was to help, Carter did not intend to rely too heavily on him. He was still concerned that the bellboy's excess energy and over-anxiousness might get in the way of his discretion.

Carter finished the remainder of his breakfast, took a shower and dressed, then walked down the hall to pay

Miss Megan Ward a visit. He didn't anticipate any problems convincing her that he was who he said he was. If she worked in central filing of AXE, there should be a way for him to make her believe his identity—that is, if she didn't recognize him as soon as he showed up at her door.

Carter had only seen a head-and-shoulders shot of Megan Ward in David Hawk's office, so he was not quite prepared for the rest of her. When she opened the door in reply to his knock, he was stunned into momentary silence. It was not that she was an extraordinary beauty, but there was something about her in person that did not come across in a picture. She was about five feet six, carried herself gracefully, and had high, proud breasts, and a trim waist.

"Yes?" she asked tentatively. "Can I help you?"

"Uh, yes, Miss Ward," Carter said. "Could I come in and talk to you for a moment?"

"Uh, I don't know," she said, eyeing him curiously. "I don't know you—"

"Are you sure?"

She frowned at him and said, "Well, now that you mention it, you do look kind of familiar . . ."

"You've probably seen me, or a photo of me, where you work, in the Amalgamated Press Building on Dupont Circle."

It came to her then. He could see it in her eyes first, and then her mouth opened in surprise.

"You're—"

"Could we talk about it inside?" he asked, cutting her off.

"Of course," she said. "Of course. Please come in."

He looked up and down the hall to satisfy himself that no one was watching, then entered her suite.

"You're Nick Carter!" she blurted out when they were inside.

"That's right."

"I know all about you," she said, excitement causing her face to flush.

"Do you?"

"Well, I mean, I've read the files—"

"Are you supposed to read them or file them?" he teased.

"Well, I have to read them in order to file them, don't I?" she asked, on the defensive and a little worried.

"Yeah, I guess you do," he replied with a grin, and she relaxed.

"I had no idea you were on the island, Mr. Carter."

"My name is Taylor," he said, "Nick Taylor, as long as we're on this island together. Okay?"

"Oh, of course," she said, looking very serious. "I understand."

"But you can call me Nick."

"All right, Nick."

"Megan, let's sit down. I have to talk to you about something," he said.

"Sure," she said, and they moved to the couch in the center of the room.

"Is this about what's going on here in Santa Caribe? The coup?" she asked.

"That's exactly what it's about," Carter answered.

"That's why I'm here, to help the right people get into office."

"Why have you come to see me?"

"You're the only one of our people on this island," Carter told her. "We took enough of a chance sending me in, but we can't risk sending anyone else. If anyone finds out that the United States is tampering with this country's internal affairs, it would be very bad."

"I understand," she said solemnly, "but what happens if you get caught?"

"No one in our government will admit that he knows me or why I'm here."

Her eyes widened, and then she asked again, "Why have you come to me?"

"For help."

"From me?" she asked, surprised. "What can I do?"

"Right now, I don't know," Carter said. "I just want to know if you'll be available if I need you."

"I suppose so."

"You don't have to help me, you know," Carter said, "but I'll try not to ask you to do anything that would be dangerous. That's what I get paid for."

"Well, we work for the same people, right?" she asked.

"But we don't do the same things," he answered.

"We probably do what we do for the same reasons, Nick. I wanted to work for the government to do what I could to help my country. I assume that you've been sent here to help Santa Caribe because it will end up helping our country as well."

"You're right about that, Megan."

"Then I want to help," she said. "I'll do whatever you ask me to do."

Carter didn't run across those kinds of pure motives very often. His world had become very mercenary, and this lovely young woman was like a breath of fresh air.

"As I said, Megan, right now I don't know what I want you to do. You've been here for some time now, haven't you?"

She nodded and said, "A couple of weeks. I was only supposed to be here for a week, but since the president was assassinated, no one can leave the island.

"I want you to think," he said. "Think about anything you might have heard on the streets, in shops, or in restaurants, both before and after the assassination. You might have heard something that will help us, even if you didn't realize it at the time."

"All right. How do I get in touch with you if I think of something?"

"I'm in room four-oh-five, right down the hall," he said, "but we're going to have to arrange something so that we can meet outside as well."

"You mean like pretending we're interested in each other?" she asked, smiling.

"Probably," he said, returning her smile, "if that won't be too hard for you to pretend."

"Oh, no," she said, "it wouldn't be a problem at all."

"Well, I'm glad to hear that. Did you have any plans for today?"

"Nothing much, just what I've done every day that I've been here," she said. "I go swimming either on the beach or in the pool."

"Why don't you go down to the pool, and then I'll come along and we'll strike up a conversation. From there we'll have lunch together, and after that no one should be surprised to see us together."

"All right," she said, standing up. "I'll put on my suit and go down."

"Fine," he said, also rising. "I'll see you down there—and remember to let me make the first move."

"That won't be hard," she said. "I'm usually very shy about . . . forming attachments."

"I find that very hard to believe," he said. "You're a very lovely woman, Megan."

"Just remember one thing, Mr. Nick . . . Taylor," she warned him.

"What's that?"

"I've read your files," she said. "Like I said before, I know all about you. I've read about your . . . escapades with women."

"Escapades?" he said. "I'd hardly call them that."

"Well, you have a reputation, and people with reputations usually feel that they have to live up to them."

"Well, I think you've got me pegged wrong, Megan," he told her, "but I'll remember what you said."

"If I'm wrong, I'll apologize," she said, "but where there's smoke, somebody usually ends up getting burned."

"That's very profound," Carter said. "I'll be sure to keep that in mind too."

"What are you going to do now?" she asked, walking him to the door.

"Well, I want to act a little bit like a tourist. Are they stopping everyone who walks through the streets?"

"Not until after dark," she answered.

"Then I think I'll walk around some—and keep my own ears open—before I come back to the hotel for a dip and some lunch. After all," he said, "you never know who you might meet around the pool."

All Carter found out that morning was that he couldn't go ten steps without seeing a soldier armed with an M-16. Everywhere he went he was under surveillance, only it wasn't just him, it was everyone on the island, tourists and residents alike. Mahbee couldn't afford to trust anyone. He probably had his soldiers watching one another as well. Carter wondered how many bodyguards the ex-bodyguard had around himself.

He took a walk down by the docks, but there were more soldiers there than anywhere else, and they wouldn't let him by.

"Forbidden," one placid-faced black man said to him, holding his M-16 at chest level, and Carter nodded and retreated. He was supposed to have been on the island for a couple of weeks and should have known that the docks were off limits. He didn't want to press the matter and arouse the guard's suspicions. The island's tiny airstrip would likewise be guarded, and he decided not to go near it. He did not want to be described to Mahbee as having tried to get near both places in the same day.

He went back to the hotel, changed into his bathing trunks, and, putting a towel over his shoulder, went down to the pool.

There were plenty of people around the pool, and many of them were paired off, so it wouldn't be too

58

difficult to "pick up" Megan Ward. Santa Caribe seemed to be a big honeymoon spot, which meant that Megan had picked the wrong place to go on her vacation.

He spotted her across the pool, executing an almost perfect backstroke. He waited for her to get out of the pool and walk to a chaise longue, and then, while she was drying her hair, he walked to the empty chair next to hers, dropped his towel onto it, and dove into the pool. He swam the length of the pool a couple of times, then got out and went back to dry off. Megan was lying down now, eyes closed, face raised to the sun, when a waiter came over and asked Carter if he wanted a drink.

"Yes," Carter said, "something cold and with rum in it, I think."

"Very good, sir."

"Hold on a second," he told the waiter. This was a good time to approach Megan, with the waiter as a witness. "Perhaps this young lady would also like a drink. I'd be happy to buy her one."

Megan took her cue, raised her sunglasses, and looked over at Carter with a curious look on her face.

"How about it?" Carter asked.

"Sure," she answered him, then said to the waiter, "Something cold and with rum in it sounds good to me, too."

"Very good, miss," the waiter said, then executed a little bow and went to fetch their drinks.

Carter sat down on his chaise longue. "My name is Nick Taylor," he said, extending his hand to her.

She took his hand in a firm grip. "Megan Ward."

"From the States?"

"Yes."

"So am I."

There were people seated at nearby chairs, and even if they couldn't hear the conversation, it would be obvious to them that Carter and Megan were meeting for the first time.

Carter settled back in his chair, and Megan said in a low voice, "Can anyone hear us?"

"Even if they can't," Carter said, "the setup is perfect. Eventually we'll move to a table for lunch, and we'll be able to talk more freely there."

"All right."

"Are you here alone?" Carter asked in a louder voice.

"Yes," Megan answered. "I guess I chose the wrong place for a vacation. I had no idea that Santa Caribe was a honeymoon paradise."

There was probably more truth in that statement than not, Carter thought.

"Not too many unattached men around, huh?"

Megan looked at him and, with a slight grin, said, "Not until now, anyway."

At that point the waiter came back with their drinks, and they enjoyed their fruit-filled rum concoctions and talked a little longer until Carter proposed that they have lunch together.

"That sounds like a marvelous idea."

"Great," Carter said. "Do you want to change before we eat?"

"Not unless you do."

"You look wonderful, and I'm comfortable as is,"

Carter said. Actually, the temperature was already in the high 90s, and he didn't want to wear more than his trunks.

"Let's go get a table, then," she said. She swung her extremely shapely legs off the lounge chair and stood up. She was wearing a black, one-piece bathing suit, cut high at the thigh and plunging in front, showing off the curves of her rounded breasts. She really did look wonderful, and it made Carter wish that they truly were on vacation.

Maybe later. . . .

SIX

George Mahbee received the message later that afternoon while he was sitting at former President Makumbo's desk, in former President Makumbo's office in the Presidential Building. True, he was not yet the president of Santa Caribe, but that was merely a formality. As soon as he hunted down the bulk of the Makumbo supporters from the hills outside of Caribe City, he would be assured of attaining the position officially.

The message was from the captain of the guard down at the docks of Caribe City. It seemed that a man had attempted to enter the dock area.

"Did he offer any resistance?" Mahbee asked.

"None, sir," the captain answered. "One of my men told him it was forbidden, and he left immediately."

"Why would someone who has been on this island for the past week, at least, need to be told that the docks were off limits?" Mahbee mused aloud.

"I don't know, sir."

"I wasn't asking you, you idiot," Mahbee snapped. "Why did it take you so long to call me with this information?"

"I only just learned it from the guard involved, sir," the man replied nervously.

"See that the man is punished for not reporting the incident promptly."

"Yes, sir."

"And captain . . ."

"Yes, sir?"

"If I do not approve of the punishment, you will be punished accordingly."

"I understand, sir."

"That's all," Mahbee said and slammed the phone down.

"Duncan!" he shouted, and a gigantic black man who dwarfed even the robust Mahbee entered the room as if he had been waiting just outside the door for his master's call.

"Yes, sir?"

One thing Mahbee knew he could always be sure of was Duncan's loyalty. Duncan had been driving the limousine the day Mahbee killed Makumbo, and he did so on the promise from Mahbee that he would then become his assistant and bodyguard, which appeared to be all that the massive, slow-witted Duncan wanted out of life.

"Our Russian friend, has he been accommodated?"

"Yes, sir."

"Bring a message to him, please, that I would like to speak to him as soon as possible."

"Yes, sir."

"In his own time, please, Duncan," Mahbee cautioned the giant. "I know how your overzealousness can sometimes cost a man his right arm."

"Yes, sir," Duncan said, and he left to do his master's bidding.

Mahbee knew that had he not cautioned Duncan, the massive man would have grabbed their Russian ally by the arm and dragged him to the Presidential Building. That would not do. The Russians were to be Mahbee's friends, and their representative would have to be treated gently, very gently, indeed.

The Russian representative was General Leo Valniev, Russia's counterpart to Nick Carter since the death of Alexi Ivanoff in Canada while he, Carter, and others were hunting the dreaded Mendoza Manuscript. Following that affair, Valniev had become the Soviet Union's number one boy.

Valniev, however, had felt that this mission was not befitting his position. Being sent to this flyspeck of a country was not his idea of a first-rate assignment. Small were the chances that he would ever run into someone like Nick Carter in this place. Was he being punished for something? He had no idea that the sweet, young blonde he had been, uh, seeing was the daughter of a high-ranking Politburo official. Besides, it had been she who had stalked him, and not the other way around. Surely a man should not be punished for not being able to run fast enough to escape the clutches of an oversexed teen-age girl.

However, upon his arrival on Santa Caribe, it had

become apparent to him that perhaps this was meant to be a vacation. This fellow, George Mahbee, seemed to have the situation well in hand and would soon lead this backward little country, thereby cementing Russia's rights to trade with Santa Caribe. Valniev did not know exactly what this country had that would be so important to the world's major powers, but that was of no concern to him. He had been sent here to observe and advise. And at the moment, Mahbee seemed in little need of advice, and the only observing Valniev was doing was around the pool at the Hotel Caribe.

He had been lying on a chaise longue off in a corner, wearing gray-lensed sunglasses, when he spotted the young woman in the black bathing suit. He had been watching her for some time and had also been about to approach her when he saw the man. Suddenly he was very alert, and the assignment in Santa Caribe took on an entirely new light. It did not even bother him that the man moved right in on the woman and got to her first. What was most important was the man himself.

Valniev had been watching the two have lunch when a waiter approached him with a written message. He opened the envelope and read the sheet inside, then crumpled it in his fist and got up. He looked again at the table where the couple was eating. The man was very intent on the woman and was seated with his back to the pool, so he could not see the barrel-chested Soviet agent walk from the pool area back into the hotel.

A moment of carelessness, Nick Carter, Valniev thought, *and one that I will allow to go by.* No doubt the American had entertained the same thoughts concerning this assignment that had passed through Valniev's mind, but now the Russian had a distinct advantage on his opposite number.

Leo Valniev knew that Nick Carter was on Santa Caribe, but the American, aware as he probably was that there was a Russian agent on the island, had no idea that his opponent was perhaps the only man in the world of espionage with the talent and ability to do what to date had been impossible.

Leo Valniev always knew that he would be the man to finally kill Nick Carter.

Nick Carter deserved no less.

George Mahbee was surprised that Valniev appeared at his office so promptly. Mahbee prided himself on the ability to read people, and he had read the Russian as a man who moved at his own speed in his own good time.

What had moved him to respond so quickly? *Perhaps*, Mahbee thought, *the man recognizes my own charisma and is responding to it. Yes, that must be it. . . .*

"Ah, my Russian friend," Mahbee said, rising behind the desk. "Come in, come in, sit down."

Valniev did not like Mahbee. He realized, however, that the man was powerful, clever, and ruthless, but he also recognized that, despite his appearance, the man was not refined enough to deserve to be on the same island—or in the same world—with Leo Valniev and Nick Carter. The man was crude, and Valniev hoped he would have to deal with him as little as possible.

Now, however, the entire situation had changed; this assignment would be a battle of wits between Valniev and Carter.

This suited Valniev perfectly.

"I believe you wanted to see me, comrade," Valniev said, taking a seat. When it was necessary, he was able to speak English without a trace of accent. In fact, he had once spent three months in Texas, and everyone he had come in contact with had been convinced that he was a native Texan. Now, however, in the presence of Mahbee, he allowed his Russian accent to come through—a constant reminder to the man behind the desk of who he was, and who he represented.

"I did, indeed," Mahbee said. "I've received a disturbing report from one of my men, and I thought I would relay it to you and see what you thought of it."

"I'm flattered," Valniev said. "Please continue."

Mahbee told him about the man who had attempted to get onto the docks, and he explained why that should be strange.

"What did the man look like?" Valniev asked.

"I, uh, don't know exactly," Mahbee said. He was fuming inside because he was embarrassed by the question, but like a true leader of men, he blamed the captain of the guard for not giving him a description and not himself for not asking for one.

"Why don't you call that soldier and ask him?" Valniev suggested.

"An excellent idea."

He called the soldier he had spoken to earlier and got a description of the man in question, which he then related to Valniev.

"Dark-haired, well-built, late thirties, early forties," Mahbee said. "Could be a lot of men."

"Or it could be Nick Carter," Valniev said, although he was quite positive that it was indeed AXE's Killmaster.

"Who is that?"

"The finest agent that the United States has. A very talented and dangerous man."

"He's your enemy, then," Mahbee said, "and you sound as if you admire the man."

"I admire excellence in any form," Leo Valniev said, "and as far as the world of espionage goes, Nick Carter—and myself—have established the standards by which other agents are measured."

"If this man, Nick Carter, is that dangerous, then perhaps you will need help," Mahbee said. "I could have Duncan—"

"Begging your pardon, President Mahbee," Valniev interrupted, using the title to flatter the man, "but Nick Carter would eat your man for breakfast and spit out the bones for lunch."

"Then perhaps you should call for help from your own country—"

"You misunderstand me, Mr. President," Valniev said. "I said that Carter was dangerous. That is not meant to imply that I cannot handle him."

"But I thought—"

"We are almost evenly matched," the Russian said, paying—to his mind—the ultimate compliment to the American, "but the operative word here is 'almost.' No, I shall not need any assistance in taking care of Nick Carter."

"But if he is here to help the Makumbo supporters—"

"He will not have time to interfere with your operations, Mr. President," Valniev assured the man. "You continue to handle your enemies, which you have been doing so admirably, and I will handle Nick Carter."

He rose from his chair and said, "Things are working out perfectly for us, Mr. President."

"I hope so."

Valniev walked to the door, then turned and said, "Unfortunately for them, however, I cannot say the same for your enemies . . . and mine." He said good-by and left the office, glad to be away from the power-hungry oaf.

Valniev thought of Nick Carter not actually as his enemy, but as more of an adversary. He had nothing personal against the man. Indeed, in another world they'd have been friends, of this he was quite sure.

Of course, that would not keep him from killing Nick Carter when the time came.

And the time was very close at hand.

"Okay, can we talk now?" Megan asked when she and Carter had their lunches in front of them. "The waiter won't be back until we call him or until our plates are empty."

"We have been talking."

"We've been playacting," Megan insisted, "and I have to tell you, it's been a strain. I don't know how you've gone through most of your life playing roles."

"Actors and actresses do it," he reminded her.

"Yes, but only their livelihoods depend on it," she argued, "not their lives."

"You'd make a terrible spy."

"I agree," she said, "but I make one hell of a file clerk."

"You could be so much more—" Carter began, but he noticed that she was no longer looking at him; her eyes were focused on something in the distance. "Did you just spot another unattached male?" he asked.

"I spotted him before," she said, "when he spotted me. I felt like I was being measured, weighed, and graded. He's leaving now." She squinted and said, "I could swear he was looking over here, but I couldn't tell with those sunglasses . . ."

"Where is he?" Carter asked, starting to turn.

"He's going in . . . there, see him?"

Carter didn't see him full face—he glimpsed first a profile and then his back—but he saw enough.

"I take back what I said," he told her.

"About what?"

"About you not making a good spy."

"Why?"

He didn't hear her last question because he was staring at the door the man had gone through. He was very surprised to find that the man the Russians had sent in on this was Leo Valniev, their very best.

The fight for Santa Caribe was really shaping up now, he thought, into something very interesting indeed.

The more George Mahbee thought about Nick Carter, the more convinced he became that the man was far too dangerous to be allowed to roam about Caribe City freely. The Russian, Valniev, obviously had great respect for the man's abilities, as well as great confidence in his own ability to handle him, but Mahbee wasn't satisfied with that.

He wanted Nick Carter taken care of, eliminated.

He called in Duncan and gave the big man specific instructions, speaking very slowly and carefully so that the dull giant would be able to follow and understand every word. When he had dismissed him, Mahbee leaned back and clasped his hands behind his head, pleased that the problem had now been taken care of.

Duncan may not have been very intelligent, but once he got a man in his clutches, there was no way out. So the problem of Nick Carter was solved, just like that. Now only the other problem, the main one, still existed. The people in the hills. Their hiding place still could not be found, and how could the Russian help them in that? In fact, what good would the Russian be now that the American was taken care of?

He would have to tolerate the Russian, but perhaps he could keep him busy. Yes, perhaps some female companionship might keep Leo Valniev from meddling in Mahbee's affairs.

After all, what help did Mahbee need from the Russian now? He had the hill people on the run—it was only a matter of time before he found where they had hidden their leader—and Nick Carter was no longer a problem.

Not after Duncan got through with him.

SEVEN

"Let's go in," Carter suggested after lunch.

"Together?"

"It'll look natural," he assured her.

"If you say so."

"An unattached man meets a beautiful woman on a Caribbean island," he recited, "buys her a drink, buys her lunch, and then they go back into the hotel together. It's a natural progression."

"What comes next?" she asked.

"That," he said, "depends on the man and the woman."

"I see."

"Come on," he said, "I'll walk you to your room."

"Are you going to tell me about that man?" she asked.

"Later," he said, and then the waiter came, and they once again started their "playacting," as Megan called it, while Nick Taylor signed the check.

73

"Can I walk you to your room?" Carter asked Megan in front of the waiter.

"Of course," Megan replied, "isn't that the natural progression of things?"

Carter gave her a look, then took her hand and led her into the hotel.

When they got to Megan's door Carter said, "Are you going to invite me in?"

"Is that also the natural prog—"

"That's the only way you're going to find out about your admirer by the pool," he broke in.

"Then by all means you're invited in, Mr. Taylor."

"Oh, just call me Nick."

She unlocked the door and they went inside.

"So," she said, dropping her towel and robe on the couch, "tell me."

"Well, I didn't get a real good look at the man," Carter said, "but from what I did see I'd swear that it was Leo Valniev."

"Leo . . ." she started to say as if she was trying to remember the name, and then she did, ". . . Valniev! I know that name. He's Russia's biggest spy, isn't he?"

"Biggest and best."

"Sort of your Russian counterpart, isn't he?"

"That's flattering," Carter said. "Leo's really very good—"

"Do you know him?"

"We've met a few times, yes," Carter said.

"You mean you've crossed swords a few times, don't you?" she asked excitedly.

"I wouldn't put it that way."

"I would," she said. "Tell me, who came out on top all those times, you or him?"

Carter thought it over a moment and then said, "It's a tie, I think. We're pretty evenly matched."

"You sound as if you have a lot of respect for the man."

"Oh, I do, but don't get me wrong," Carter said. "Officially, he's the enemy, and I'll do what I have to do to stop him."

"What about unofficially?"

"Unofficially?" Carter repeated. "I guess unofficially he's simply an opponent, an adversary."

"You mean like in checkers or something?"

"Chess would be more like it."

"What does this mean to your assignment, then?"

"It means it's going to be a little harder. I've only got one edge."

"What's that?"

"If he didn't recognize me . . ." Carter began, but he discounted that possibility almost immediately. "No, that's no good. I can't count on that."

"Why not?"

"He's too much of a pro," Carter explained. "If he was watching you—which, by the way, shows that he still has excellent taste in women—then he was bound to have seen me."

"That means he watched both of us for a while, because he didn't get up and leave until we were having lunch."

"Right, right," Carter said. "He knows I'm here, but he just might think that I don't know he's here. That gives me an edge again."

"What kind of an edge?"

"Well, if he thinks that *he* has an edge, and he doesn't, then that gives *me* an edge."

Megan touched her forehead as if she were feeling dizzy. "I don't know if I can follow that."

"Well, luckily you don't have to," he said. "I'm the one who has to worry."

"You don't mind if I worry a little, too, do you?" she asked. "Like, about you?"

"No, Megan," Carter said, taking a few steps to bring himself close to her, "I don't mind that at all."

"Nick."

"What?"

"What would the natural progression of things be in this situation?" she asked, tentatively putting her hands flat against his chest.

"Oh," he said, "I imagine something like this," and he pulled her close, crushing her breasts against his chest and kissing her.

"And next?" she asked breathlessly after the kiss.

He touched the straps of her bathing suit, then lowered them until the suit was bunched around her waist and her hardened nipples were scraping his bare chest.

"This is next," he said, lifting her in his arms. He carried her into the bedroom and gently put her down on the bed. She watched with admiration as he removed the clothes from his muscular body, and then he lowered himself onto the bed with her.

"Show me," she whispered, "show me what's next and next and next . . ."

He silenced her with a kiss and allowed his right

76

hand to stray between her legs. She was already moist, and when he began expertly touching her, she gasped into his mouth and lifted her hips off the bed.

"Oh, God," she said, sliding her mouth away from his. Undaunted, he ran his lips over her neck and then down to her breats, where he teased her nipples with his tongue, then bit them tenderly.

"Oh, Nick, please," she said, pressing herself against his hand, "please, now. I can't wait."

He slid his hand free and lifted one leg over her, positioning himself above her. Megan slid her hands down his body and then guided him into her. With his first thrust she gasped aloud and wrapped her legs around his waist. They took a few seconds to find the proper tempo, and then time and place melted away into something wonderful until they both floated back to earth after a mutually shattering climax.

After Carter left Megan Ward's room, feeling pleasantly exhausted, he went back to his room to take a shower and get dressed. Then he called room service, ordered a bottle of bourbon, and asked that Ollie bring it up. Ollie appeared at the door fifteen minutes later, beaming happily.

"Your bourbon, sir," he said, entering the room. As he put the bottle down he asked, "You finished the other bottle already?"

"No, Ollie, I didn't finish it," Carter said. "I just needed to talk to you."

"I am at your service, as always," Ollie said formally, but he ruined the formality by breaking into a grin again.

"All right, you can relax, Ollie," Carter said. "Sit down, I've got another job for you."

"Like finding Miss Ward?" Ollie asked. "A pleasant job like that I can always handle."

"It's the same kind of job, but I'm afraid it's not quite as pleasant," Carter said. "This time I want you to find out about a man who is registered in the hotel."

"What's his name?"

"His name is Leo Valniev, but he will not be registered under that name."

"A Russian spy!" Ollie exclaimed.

"A man I'm looking for," Carter said, looking Ollie in the eye, "discreetly."

"I understand perfectly," Ollie said, giving him a conspiratorial look.

"I simply want to find out what room he's in," Carter said, ignoring the look, "and that's all, Ollie. Bring me that information and you'll have been a great help." Carter then went on to describe the man in detail.

"Have no fear, Mr. Taylor," Ollie said. "You will have the information very soon."

"Just be careful," Carter said. "Don't let the man know what's happening. There's no reason for you to come in contact with him. Just use the fact that you're a hotel employee to find out if he's registered."

"I know what to do," Ollie assured him.

Carter was tired of cautioning the teen-ager, but when dealing with Valniev, you couldn't be too careful.

"Okay, Ollie," Carter said, "go ahead and bring

me the info when you get it. If I'm not around, just wait for me. Don't write anything down.''

''Never!'' Ollie said, stiffening. ''You can count on me, Nick.''

Shaking his head, Carter said, ''I know I can. Just be careful.''

After he left, Carter went and got the open bottle of bourbon and poured himself a drink. If Valniev had any inkling that Ollie was asking about him, the boy's life wouldn't be worth that proverbial nickel. *Come on, Ollie,* he thought, *just sneak a peek at the registration forms and get out. . . .*

Carter thought briefly about Alexi Ivanoff who, like Valniev, had been Russia's finest. Alexi and Carter had actually been friends of a sort, and Carter felt an odd sense of loss when the Russian was killed in Canada while trying to obtain the Mendoza Manuscript. He was glad, however, that he had never been assigned to kill Alexi, but that didn't mean that he wouldn't have if he'd been ordered to.

Just as he would not hesitate to kill Leo Valniev if it came down to that, because he knew damned well that the Russian would never hesitate to kill him.

When the bellboy showed up at Leo Valniev's door, the Russian had been expecting such a visit.

''Yes?'' he asked.

''Compliments of the management,'' Ollie said, and he held up a bottle of champagne.

''Oh?'' Valniev asked, masking his Russian accent. ''For any particular reason?''

Obviously the bellboy had not thought that far ahead. Valniev was really disappointed in the quality of the help Nick Carter had enlisted. The appearance of the bellboy with the sudden ''gift'' from the management was all Valniev needed to tell him that he no longer had an edge on his American counterpart. Somehow Carter had found out that he was on the island and was attempting to determine whether or not he was registered in the same hotel.

''Uh—'' the bellboy began helplessly.

''Forget it,'' Valniev said. ''Just put it down somewhere.''

''Yes, sir,'' the bellboy said, and then he smiled, showing those glorious white teeth. He put the bottle on a table near the door.

When Ollie turned around, Valniev was practically standing on top of him, and the boy almost panicked until he saw the five dollar bill the man was holding out to him.

''Oh, uh, thank you, sir,'' Ollie said, accepting the tip.

''Anything else?'' Valniev asked when the bellboy made no attempt to leave.

''No, uh, no, nothing else, sir,'' Ollie said. ''Enjoy the champagne.''

''I will,'' Valniev said, ''if I can find a woman to share it with.''

''You want a woman?'' Ollie asked. ''Or a young girl?''

''No, thank you,'' Valniev said, ''I will get my own. If that is all, you can go.''

''Yes, sir, I'm on my way.''

"And tell the, uh, hotel's manager that I appreciate his thoughtfulness," Valniev said.

"Yes, sir, I will tell him."

Valniev ushered Ollie out the door and shut it behind him, shaking his head.

Could Nick Carter get that desperate?

When there was a knock on Carter's door, he figured it would have to be either Megan or Ollie. He didn't think it would be Megan, because she might think that coming to his room was against rule one of the Spy Manual.

It was Ollie, smiling more brightly than ever.

"I have your information," he said happily.

"Already?"

"I said you could trust me."

Ollie entered the room and Carter shut the door behind them, then turned to face him.

"What room is he in?"

"He's upstairs on the fifth floor, room five-oh-seven—almost directly above you."

Before he could catch himself, Carter looked up, then jerked his head back down.

"You're sure?"

"A large man with a chest like this," Ollie said, holding his arms out in a circle in front of him.

"Yes, that's Leo," Carter said. Then he frowned and asked, "How did you find him?"

"I checked the registrations just prior to the assassination," Ollie said, "and I talked to the desk clerks. One of them remembered a man fitting the Russian's description, and when I showed him the registration cards, he remembered his name." Ollie grinned, proud of his detective work. "After that, I went to his room."

"You did what?" Carter exploded.

"I went up to his room," Ollie said. "I brought him a bottle of champagne, compliments of the management."

"A bottle of champagne," Carter muttered. "What was the occasion?"

"That's funny," Ollie said. "He asked me the same question."

"And what did you tell him?"

"Uh—"

"Thats what I thought," Carter said, shaking his head. "Ollie, is that your idea of being discreet?"

"I was only trying to help," Ollie protested. "Don't worry, Nick, he didn't suspect a thing. He even tipped me five dollars."

"Yeah, well, he tipped me, too," Carter growled.

"Huh?"

"Forget it. Go on back to work, Ollie."

"You'll call me if you need more help?"

"You can bet on it."

When Ollie was gone, Carter grabbed the bourbon and poured himself a stiff drink. One thing was now certain: any edge he might have had on Leo Valniev was gone, thanks to Ollie the well-meaning bellboy.

Of course, the thing that bothered Carter the most was that Valniev might think that he had actually sent Ollie up there with that bottle of champagne.

Carter would never get that sloppy. He hoped that Valniev would think it over and realize that fact.

● ● ●

At that moment, one floor up and one room over, Leo Valniev was thinking exactly that. Nick Carter would never be that incompetent, which meant that it had been the Makumbo people. Perhaps he should not have allowed the bellboy to leave his room alive.

Perhaps he was getting soft.

If the Makumbo faction knew Valniev was here, so did Nick Carter. Perhaps it was time for a face-to-face with the American, since it was now obvious that each knew about the other. It was foolish to go on pretending that they didn't.

EIGHT

Nick Carter called Megan's room, and when she answered he said, "It's Nick Taylor."

"Oh," she said, a little slow on the uptake, but she finally got there. "Hello, Mr. Taylor."

"Now, now, I thought we were beyond that," he scolded her.

"I guess we are—Nick," she replied.

"I was wondering if you'd like to have dinner with me tonight?"

"Where?"

"Where else? With the curfew it's either the hotel dining room, your room, or mine."

"Let's try the dining room," she said. "After that we can just follow the natural progression of things."

"I'm for that," Carter said. "I'll pick you up in your room at about seven."

"Fine. See you then."

At five minutes to seven Carter knocked on Megan's

85

door, and when she answered they headed straight for the dining room.

In the elevator she asked, ''Do you think your phone is tapped?''

''It's possible,'' he said. ''They could have bugged my room as well. We'll have to go on being Megan Ward and Nick Taylor except when we're in your room.''

''My room?'' she asked, smiling.

''And maybe even then,'' he added. ''We'll just have to go on acting as if we're really interested in each other.''

''I'll try and force myself.''

They kept up the act for the benefit of the waiter, but once they had been served their entrees, dropped it and spoke in low tones.

''I've verified the fact that the man from the pool this afternoon is who I thought it was.''

''What does that mean?''

''It means we're dealing with the very best instead of just an egomaniac of a would-be ruler of a tiny country.''

''So what are you going to do now? Do the two of you circle each other like a couple of wounded bears?''

''Wounded bears?''

''Or whatever kind of animals circle each other,'' Megan impatiently said. ''You know what I mean.''

''Yeah, I do, and I think maybe Leo and I ought to sit down and have a talk about this.''

''You and the Russian are going to sit down and talk?''

"What's wrong with that?"

"Won't he try to kill you or something?"

"Not unless he's got a damned good reason," Carter said, "and right now I don't have any reason to kill him, so I don't think he's got any reason to kill me—yet."

"That's encouraging," Megan said. "The 'yet,' I mean. That means that eventually you will be trying to kill each other."

"It's a possibility," Carter explained, "not an eventuality."

"Wonderful."

Carter picked up his glass of wine but stopped when he saw the look on Megan's face as she looked past him.

"What is it?" he asked.

"Speak of the devil . . ."

". . . and up he pops?"

She nodded. "And he's coming this way."

"Relax," Carter told her. "If I've been thinking about having a talk, the odds are that he has too. Just relax, listen, and look pretty. That last one ought to be a cinch for you."

"Thanks."

"Ah, my friend," Valniev's voice said from behind Carter as a heavy hand fell on his shoulder. "How good to see you here."

Carter looked up and smiled and said, "Well, hello . . ."

"But surely you remember me, my friend," Valniev said. "Walter Horst."

"Wally Horst," Carter said, standing up and putting out his hand. "Of course. It's been a long time. How are you?"

"Fine, just fine," Valniev said. "I hope I am not disturbing your dinner."

"Not at all," Carter said. "In fact, why don't you sit down and join us?"

"Precisely what I was hoping you would suggest," the Russian said. With a bow to Megan he pulled out one of the empty chairs and sat down.

"I see you and your lovely companion have just started to eat," he said. "I won't stay long." Valniev lowered his voice then and added, "I thought it was time we had a talk."

"I was thinking the same thing," Carter said, and he looked pointedly at Megan and said, "but not here."

"My room?" Valniev asked.

"Nope," Carter said. "The beach. We'll meet at the pool and walk on the beach."

"How romantic," Valniev said. "It is too bad we must leave behind this beautiful young lady, yes?"

"Too bad indeed," Carter said. He turned to Megan and said, "It's business, honey. You wouldn't be interested."

Megan took the cue, batted her eyelashes at Valniev, and said, "I just have no head at all for business."

"But such a lovely head," the Russian said. Looking at Carter he said, "I will leave you to your dinner and to your charming companion. Ten o'clock, by the pool?"

Carter looked at Megan, than back at Valniev and said, "How about eleven?"

Valniev looked at Megan, then looked at Carter and smiled. "Of course." He turned to Megan and said, "Enjoy your dinner, miss—it was my pleasure to have met you."

"Why, thank you. You're very kind."

"Until later," Valniev said to Carter, and then he turned and left the dining room.

"He's very charming," Megan remarked.

"And deadly," Carter said. "Let's not forget the deadly."

After they had finished their dessert and coffee, Carter took Megan back to her room, but he only stopped in for a moment.

"Can't you . . . stay?" she asked hesitantly.

He moved closer and took hold of her shoulders.

"I've got to meet Leo," he said, then paused and corrected himself. "I mean Wally. But I could come back later."

"I wish you would," Megan said, putting her hands on his chest. "That way I'd know you were all right."

"Oh, I'll be all right," he assured her. "I'm just going to talk to him."

"Maybe you trust him," Megan said, "but I don't."

"I didn't say I trusted him," Carter said, "but Leo's a pro. He's not going to kill me without a reason."

"What if he has a reason that you don't know about?"

"Like what?"

"I don't know 'like what,' " she said. "I'm just

89

asking a question, that's all. I'm just trying to get you to be careful."

"That's something I decided for myself a long, long time ago, Megan," Carter told her. "I'm always careful with two kinds of people."

"And they are . . . ?"

He tweaked her nose and said, "Spies and women."

Carter got to the pool area early, hoping to get there first, but that was not to be.

"Ah, my friend Nick," Valniev said as Carter came out of the hotel. "How good of you to come."

"Leo," Carter greeted the Russian. "It's a bit of a surprise to find you here."

"Also you," Valniev said. "Shall we walk on the beach and discuss our mutual surprise?"

"By all means."

As they walked down to the beach Valniev asked, "What about your lovely companion?"

"She's waiting for me in her room."

"I must tell you, my friend, I'm impressed."

"With what?"

"I was stalking that lovely creature yesterday by the pool, and suddenly there you were."

"That may be the main difference between us, Leo," Carter said. "I usually act right away."

"If that is the difference between us, my friend, it is only when it comes to women, eh?"

When they got down to the beach they started walking along the damp sand, careful to avoid the incoming tide.

"I assume you're here to help Mahbee take over," Carter said bluntly.

"Ah yes, Mr. Mahbee, the man who would be king, as it were," Valniev said with a heavy sigh. "Unfortunately, my country prefers that Mahbee become the president of Santa Caribe. Personally, I have no liking or respect for the man at all, but I must do my job . . . just as you must do yours, yes?"

"That's true."

"You are here to assist the Makumbo supporters, is that not so?" Valniev asked.

"Well, I wouldn't expect to find us on the same side, would you?" Carter replied.

"Alas, no, though it would be a great pleasure to work with you for once, and not against you."

"I'd agree with that."

"Perhaps in the future, eh? If we both get off this wretched island alive."

"Is there any reason why we shouldn't?"

"At the moment, no—none," Valniev said. "But things do have a habit of taking a turn for the worse in our business."

"How much of an active role do you intend to take in this, uh, revolution?" Carter asked.

"I hadn't intended to take any sort of an active role," Valniev answered. "Mahbee seemed to have the matter well in hand when I arrived. Most of his enemies are in the hills, and it is just a matter of ferreting them out and eliminating them."

"Has that changed?"

"Drastically, with your arrival, Nick," Valniev

said. "Mahbee wouldn't have a chance with you directing the Makumbo forces."

"But I'm not directing them," Carter said.

"No? I find that hard to believe. They would be foolish not to take advantage of your knowledge and expertise."

"I'm not here to be the general of their army, Leo. I'm here for the same reason you were sent."

"To observe and advise," Valniev said.

"Exactly."

"A gross misuse of our talents, eh?"

"I expect that we'll both remain in the background while Mahbee's and Makumbo's forces continue to fight it out."

Valniev clucked his tongue at Carter the way one would at a naughty child. "Do you expect me to believe that, my friend? You know that for you to sit back and do nothing would spell defeat for your allies. No, you must try and make them listen to what you have to say, and I must try to do the same with George Mahbee—though I tend to think that I have the harder task here. The man has a head like a block of cement."

Thinking of Willem, Carter said, "I don't have all that much more to work with, Leo, believe me."

"I think we would do just as well to go somewhere quiet and have a game of chess, my friend; winner take all."

"That's what it comes down to," Carter agreed.

"Alas, that would be far too easy an answer for either side," Valniev lamented.

"Have you had enough of this sand?" Carter asked,

making a face at the amount of the stuff that had managed to creep into his shoes.

"Quite," Valniev said. "What do you say to a nightcap before we end our little meeting?"

"That's fine with me."

"A glass of good vodka before turning in."

"I'll settle for bourbon."

"Agh!" Valniev said, making a face. "I will make a vodka drinker of you yet, my friend. Mark my words."

They walked back up to the hotel and sat at the bar, and Valniev told the bartender to run a tab for him.

"The drinks will be on me," he insisted, and Carter acquiesced.

"Quite a coincidence that we're both staying at the same hotel, wouldn't you say?" Carter asked when they had their drinks in hand.

"Not really," Valniev disagreed. "After all, it is the best hotel on the island. Where else would you or I stay?"

"That's true."

To a certain extent they had been open with each other, but they were still—to use Megan's words—circling each other warily, playing the "game" of spy versus spy. Any young, would-be operatives in the world of espionage could have watched the two of them as they sat there drinking together and learned a great deal.

Valniev proposed a second round, and Carter agreed. Then the Russian said, "Well, I must not keep you from your lovely companion any longer, especially if she is waiting in her room for you. Ah,"

Valniev said dreamily, "if you had not moved in on her so soon, my friend . . ."

"There are other women on the island," Carter reminded him.

"Yes, but alas, they all seem to have new husbands with them. It is not likely that a young bride would tire of her new husband so quickly."

"Perhaps not," Carter said, "but stranger things have happened. Keep your eyes open, Leo, and be ready to turn on the charm. You still know how to do that, I assume."

"You flatter me," Valniev said.

"Not much," Carter replied.

"One more drink?"

"No, thanks," Carter said. "As you say, I do have a young lady waiting for me."

"Anxiously," Valniev added. "Go and give the lady my love, my friend. Tell her that if she tires of you, I would be happy to distract her in any way I can."

"I'll tell her."

As Carter rose Valniev said, "Put your time together to good use, Nick."

"I'm sure we will," Carter said.

"Nick," Valniev called as Carter started to turn away.

"Yes?"

"I would say that we have both moved our king's pawns to king four," Valniev said. "The game has started."

"But who is playing white, Leo?" Carter asked. "Who has the next move?"

"Ah, knowing that would make it not quite as much fun," Valniev said. He raised his glass to Carter, then tossed back its contents in one swallow.

"I'm alive," Carter said when Megan opened her door.

She drew him into the room and hugged him, saying, "It's not funny, you know. At least, it isn't to me."

"No, it's not," he said, putting his arms around her and holding her tightly. They remained that way for a few moments, and then she pulled away.

"Tell me what happened."

"Nothing," Carter said. "We walked on the beach, I got sand in my shoes, we had a few drinks, and we talked."

"You mean you fenced."

"You could put it that way," Carter said, "if you had a vivid imagination."

"Well, I have, and it's been working overtime. I think I would like you to make love to me, just so I'll know you're really here."

With uncharacteristic boldness she shrugged off her dress and stood before him clad only in a pair of panties. Her high, firm breasts were starkly white against the other, tanned portions of her body, and her nipples were already swelling perceptibly in anticipation.

Carter removed his jacket, and she closed the distance between them and began unbuttoning his shirt. In a few moments he was naked, and he knelt down on one knee to help her off with her panties. Then he stood up and they walked into the bedroom. She stretched out on the bed, and he joined her. He began to circle her nipples with his tongue, remembering how much she enjoyed it, and then he kissed each one. She moaned and clasped his head close to her chest, crushing his face to her breasts.

"Please," she whispered, "now."

This time, however, Carter did not quite bend to her will. He abandoned her breasts, moving his mouth down over her ribs to her belly and below. She raised her hips to meet the probings of his tongue, but he teasingly allowed his mouth to slide away and kiss the inside of her tan thighs.

"Oh, God, don't—" she said tightly, reaching down to grab his head and reposition it tightly against her. She began to tremble, and he moved his elbows so that they pinned her down, making her unable to move. This seemed to increase the intensity of her spasms and she wanted to scream, but she confined herself to a low, keening wail until the waves of pleasure began to subside.

"Oh, God, Nick," she gasped, "you've got to—"

"I will," he said.

As he rose above her she opened her legs for him and he sank into her. Suddenly they were pressing tightly against each other in frenzied motion, and when she came a second time, he allowed himself to go with her. . . .

"You certainly are alive," she whispered afterward.

"Thank you, and so are you." He leaned over and gave her a gentle kiss.

"Nick," she said, her tone changing suddenly.

"Hmm?"

"Aren't you afraid that my room might be bugged like yours?"

"Not yet," he said. "Leo hasn't had time. He only saw us together today. By tomorrow it probably will be. He's a pro and he'll bug the room simply as a precaution."

"Couldn't you unbug it, or debug it, whatever the term is?" she asked.

"I could, but then he would just bug it again. Besides, he won't believe much of what we say because he'll know that I know that both rooms are bugged."

"Then why bug it?"

"Because it's SOP," he said. "It's the way the game is played, even if he thinks you're no danger."

"Do you and he always play by the rules?"

"We start out that way, but somewhere along the line we both start bending them a little. We're like two chess players who have played each other so many times that we could virtually make each other's moves until about mid-game. At that point, we start using our imaginations, and it really gets interesting."

" 'Interesting,' " she repeated. "That's some way to look at danger, as something interesting."

"That's the only way to look at it."

"I suppose it is, for you." She turned toward him and nestled her head onto his shoulder. "I haven't been much help up until now."

"Sure you have," he said, putting his arm around her. "This helps."

"I mean real help," she said. "Isn't there something I can do?"

"I can't say yet, Megan, because I haven't yet decided if there's anything I can do."

"Won't you have to decide soon?"

He nodded and said, "I'll give myself one more day, and then I'll have a meeting with the Makumbo people."

"What will you do until then?" she asked.

"I don't know," he said, turning his body so that it was tightly pressed against hers. "I only know what I'll be doing for the next few hours—if it's all right with you."

She giggled. "I said I wanted to help, didn't I?

NINE

When Nick Carter left the hotel the following morning, he did not see the huge man across the street—not right away, anyway. When the man started after him and followed him for most of the morning, it was virtually impossible for a man of Carter's experience not to spot the massive tail.

Carter went to the Caribe City library and read all the articles he could find on Bili Makumbo and George Mahbee. He finished up with the stories following the assassination of Makumbo. The president had been on his way to a large rally to address his people and had been shot to death in the back seat of his limousine. His bodyguard had been knocked unconscious, as had his driver. The only odd thing was that his vice-president, Jules Berbick, was supposed to have been in the car with him; but the man was nowhere to be found either immediately after or subsequently. The man had vanished from the face of the island.

Could it be that Berbick was the man for whom Willem and his people were fighting?

Carter began to do some research on Berbick, and what he found made that seem unlikely. From all indications, Berbick was a figurehead vice-president. A do-nothing. In other words, a perfect politician. Could such a man suddenly become the force behind a fight for power and control?

Thinking about it for a moment, if it was Berbick, then he was in hiding in order to avoid an assassination attempt. Whoever the leader was, that was why he was in hiding. It didn't only apply to Jules Berbick.

Another way of looking at the situation was that Berbick could have been wounded and left for dead, and had somehow managed to crawl away into hiding. Maybe he was waiting to recover fully from his wounds before reappearing.

Still, Berbick's history didn't show much promise for a new leader.

Carter returned all the clippings he had been reading and left the library, conscious that he was still being shadowed.

The man was obviously not a professional; in fact, he seemed to be making no effort to go unnoticed.

What purpose did an obvious tail serve? None that Carter could readily see. Why would the big man be so careless about following someone unless it was just something he was unaccustomed to doing? And if this was an unusual job, why was he doing it now?

There was only one sure way to find out, and that was to ask him.

He decided the best thing to do would be to find a secluded spot, lead his tail there, and question him. But Carter didn't know the city very well, and there was only one person who could supply the location of such a spot.

Carter found a phone and called the Hotel Caribe. When the switchboard answered he asked for Ollie.

When Ollie came on, Carter said, "This is Nick Taylor, Ollie."

"Mr. Taylor," Ollie said. "Where are you?"

"I'm out walking around the city," Carter replied, "and I was wondering if you could help me with something."

"Of course," Ollie said happily. "What?"

"Do you know a place in the city where two people could go and talk where they wouldn't be disturbed?"

"Do you mean a restaurant or something like that?" Ollie asked.

"No," Carter said, "someplace outside. A court-yard, an alley—"

"For a man and a woman?"

"Two men," Carter said, "one of whom might not like the idea very much." He hoped Ollie would understand, because he didn't want to say too much more on the phone.

"I think I know what you mean, Nick," Ollie said, "and I think I know a place."

"Good, but you'll have to give me directions to it."

"Okay," Ollie said, and he went on to tell Carter what kind of place it was and how to get there on foot.

"I've got it, Ollie. Thanks."

"What's going on? Do you want me to meet you there and help—"

"No!" Carter said loudly. "Stay away from there, Ollie. I don't want you anywhere near that place, do you understand?"

"Yes, I understand," Ollie replied.

"Thanks again for the information. 'Bye."

Carter hung up before Ollie could say anything else, then checked to see if his tail was still there. When he was sure he was, he started off, following Ollie's directions to a small cul-de-sac at the end of an alley where they could have a nice little chat . . . undisturbed.

As Carter approached the mouth of the alley, he considered briefly the possibility that his tail would know about the alley and not enter, but he decided to give it a try.

He walked into the alley and could see ahead of him the cul-de-sac, which had a dry fountain in it. He walked on until he came to the fountain, then turned and waited for the other man to enter, hoping that he would.

He waited for five minutes, then ten, and still the big man didn't appear. Perhaps the man was smarter than he looked, but now the problem Carter faced was whether or not the man was waiting at the other end of the alley for him to come out.

He went back into the alley and unholstered Wilhelmina, feeling better with the Luger in his hand. A lot of people didn't like Lugers. For one thing, they had a reputation fo jamming easily and frequently, but

Carter had never had that problem with Wilhelmina.

When he was five feet from the mouth of the alley he slowed down and pressed himself against the wall. He continued on at a slower pace and then, holding the gun by his side where it would be hidden but ready, he stepped out of the alley and examined the street in both directions.

The big man was nowhere to be seen. Apparently, when Nick went into the alley, not only hadn't the man followed, he'd given up the tail.

Feeling foolish, Carter put away his gun and started off down the street. He couldn't have been wrong about the tail. The man had definitely been following him but for some reason had abandoned his mission rather abruptly.

Carter decided to go directly back to the Hotel Caribe. Perhaps the man would pick him up there and start all over again. If that were the case, Carter would have to find some other way of confronting the big goon. He doubted that the tail would have been set up by Leo Valniev. The Russian would not get that desperate for help. The man had to have been sent by Mahbee to keep an eye on Carter, which meant that Valniev had told George Mahbee about him. Being "Nick Taylor" had become an exercise in futility, because his true identity was now known. If he was going to act and do something that would help Liza, Willem, and their mysterious leader, it was going to have to be soon.

When Carter got to the hotel, he did not see the big man anywhere outside, and the same went for the lobby. He took the elevator to the fourth floor, considered stopping at Megan's room, but decided to go to his first.

As he approached his door, he took out his gun just as a precaution. He'd felt foolish about the tail, but didn't want to take any chances here. He inserted his key, then opened the door and cautiously entered the room with the gun held ahead of him.

As soon as he entered his room, a massive arm snaked around from behind and pressed against his throat, cutting off his air, and Carter knew that he had found his tail.

He reached up and tried to grab the arm with both hands, but he was unable to get his hands fully around the arm. The man was tremendous and built like an ox. Carter couldn't force his fingers between the arm and his own throat. He tried to drive his elbows back into the man's stomach, but the blows seemed to have no effect. It was like hitting a tree trunk.

As a pounding built in his ears and spots began to appear before his eyes, Carter knew that he would not be able to muscle his way out of the man's hold, so he did the only thing he could do. He jammed the barrel of Wilhelmina against one of the man's massive thighs, and pulled the trigger.

The hold on his neck was removed immediately as the man howled in pain. Released, Carter fell to the floor, but before he could fully catch his breath, one of the man's hands closed around the wrist of the hand that was holding the gun and squeezed. Carter did not want to drop the Luger, but as he felt the bones in his wrist beginning to grind together, he had no choice but to open his hand. The gun was plucked from his fingers and thrown aside, then Carter's wrist was released and the huge man knocked him down with a kick of his good leg.

Quickly getting to his feet, Carter turned to face his attacker. The massive man—the same one who had been following him—began to advance on him despite a bullet wound leaking blood from his right thigh.

Carter backed away as the giant, who was at least six and a half feet tall, closed in on him. The man was incredibly ugly, his eyes full of red veins. He was sweating hard, which could have been a result of his leg wound.

"Look, friend," Carter said, "we don't have to do this, you know, just because I shook your tail."

The man didn't answer; he just kept coming. Carter moved around so that the couch was between them, and he tried talking to him again, but the man gave no indication that he was even able to understand what was being said.

After a few seconds, Carter realized that the time for talking was over.

He didn't know where his gun was, but he still had Hugo strapped to his forearm, and that was—literally—an edge he would save until he could make the best use of it.

The only weak spot his adversary had, that Carter could see, was that thigh wound, so he came out from behind the couch, and as the man came within striking distance he launched a kick at that wound. For a big man, his attacker moved very quickly, and he was able to turn his body so that the kick glanced off the side of his wounded leg and did not hit the wound itself. Still, it must have hurt like hell, but there was no noticeable reaction from him.

Carter started to look around for something to hit the guy with, then decided on the wooden coffee table in front of the couch. He lifted it up and swung it at the man, who lifted his arm and allowed the wood to splinter harmlessly against his massive forearm.

"Jesus," Carter muttered, backpedalling a bit. He decided to wait now for the big man to rush him, at which point he would produce Hugo and try and plant him where he would do the most good—or damage. Keeping this fellow alive long enough to interrogate now seemed out of the question. When a man was that intent on killing you, you couldn't worry about keeping him alive.

"Okay, big guy," Carter said, "come and get it."

As the man started his charge, Carter flicked his wrist and Hugo slid into his hand. He sidestepped, and as the big man bounced off the wall, he drove the knife into his side. As he pulled the knife out, however, his assailant swung a backhand that caught him high on the cheek and knocked him halfway across the room. Miraculously, Carter was able to hold onto his knife, for all the good it had done him. Bleeding from his thigh and his side, the wounded man continued to advance on him.

Carter realized that, without a gun, there was only one way for him to come out of this alive. As his opponent charged at him again, Carter also moved forward, surprising him. Puzzled, the other man slowed momentarily, but it was just long enough for Carter to get around him and jump up on his back. As the man tried to shake him off, Carter grabbed hold of his hair. His weight caused the man's head to fall back, exposing his throat, and Carter laid the razor-sharp edge of Hugo against the man's skin and whipped it across.

As the blood cascaded over his chest, the big man staggered, but still Carter did not relinquish his hold on the man's hair. He remained on his back until the giant fell to his hands and knees. The man made hideous, strangling noises as his blood formed a pool on the floor, and then he fell facedown into it and lay still. Carter rolled off the man's back and away from him, then leaned over to examine the body. At that moment the man lifted an arm, and Carter jumped back, readying his knife for another thrust, but the massive body merely jerked, its eyes staring sightlessly at the carpet.

When he was sure the man was finally dead, Carter put away the knife, retrieved Wilhelmina, and then searched through the intruder's pockets. The man had a wallet, but there was nothing in it but Santa Caribe currency. There was nothing on the body that could identify it, and now all that was left was to dispose of the corpse.

Discreetly.

Which left Ollie out . . . or did it?

Carter went to the phone and called room service, and then asked if Ollie could come to the phone.

"Ollie here."

"Ollie, this is Nick Taylor."

"Hello there, Nick," the bellboy said. "What can I do for you?"

"I have to see my friend, Ollie, very quickly."

"Friend?" Ollie asked. "Which friend is that?"

"You know, the friend who recommended this hotel to me."

"Oh," Ollie said, "that friend."

"Yes, that one. It's imperative that we meet right away."

"I will let her know," Ollie said. "Is everything all right?"

"Everything's fine, Ollie," Carter said patiently. "Just deliver my message."

"Yes, sir."

Carter hung up and hoped that Ollie would simply do what he was told and not improvise. He did not even want the bellboy to know about the body for fear that he would let it slip. Carter hoped that Liza would be able to arrange for the disposal of the body.

He still had some bourbon left in the first bottle and he decided that this was a good time to drink it. There was no telling how long it would take Ollie to deliver the message, and then how long it would take Liza and Willem to act on it. Carter didn't relish spending the remainder of the day in his room with the body, but he didn't have any choice. He didn't want anyone finding out about this before he was ready. It was going to be hard enough to clean the blood off the rug without the maids noticing it. He would have liked to go down the hall and wait in Megan's room, but it was better that she didn't know about the incident either.

He sat on the couch, poured himself another drink, and settled down to wait.

TEN

One floor above, Leo Valniev had heard what he thought was a shot. True, the barrel of Carter's gun had been jammed against the attacker's thigh, but to an experienced ear—like Leo Valniev's—the sound of a shot was still recognizable, even when muffled.

"What's wrong?" the red-haired American tourist lying next to him in bed asked. She had a right to ask. One minute the Russian's strong hands were kneading her flesh, and the next minute he was sitting up in bed, listening . . . but to what?

"Nothing, my dear," he said. "I am just listening to the wind."

"To the wind?" she asked, sitting up. The sheet fell away, revealing full, pear-shaped breasts with erect, russett-colored nipples. A patch of freckles ran across the tops of her breasts and fell into the cleavage.

"Listen," he said.

He waited, listening patiently for a follow-up shot,

but when none came he decided that the single shot was worth investigating.

"Where are you going?" the redhead demanded when he stood up and began dressing.

"For a walk," he said. "You have drained me, and I need to take a short walk. I will be back."

She watched as the barrel-chested Russian dressed, and then he leaned over the bed to kiss her warmly. The feel of his lips on hers wiped away any thoughts she might have had about dressing and leaving.

"Wait for me," he said.

"Of course," she said.

He trailed his fingers across her nipples fleetingly, then left the room.

Outside in the hall he found the stairway and descended to the fourth floor. Looking out the door into the hallway, he had a clear view of the door to "Nick Taylor's" room, and he settled down to wait. If something had happened inside, there would soon be some activity to indicate to him just what had happened.

Valniev had the patience to wait and see.

He only hoped his friend upstairs was patient as well.

George Mahbee sat behind his desk, wondering what in hell was holding up his man, Duncan. He should have been back by now with Nick Carter's head in his hip pocket. If something had gone wrong, Mahbee would have Duncan's head. Mahbee had dismissed Nick Carter as a threat, and he did not want to have to be forced into taking the American into consideration again.

He stared at the phone on his desk, willing it to ring, willing Duncan to be on the other end, telling him that everything had gone off as planned.

When Willem got the message from Ollie, Liza was there with him, and she insisted on being allowed to go to the hotel to see what Carter needed.

"You said I'd be able to help Nick while he was here trying to help us," she reminded him.

"It's too dangerous," Willem insisted.

"Dangerous or not, I'm going, Willem," she said. "You have no right to keep me from making a contribution."

"Go then," he snapped, "and be damned! Go to your American friend, Nick Carter. He'll be able to do nothing for us, mark my words."

"I'll let you know what he needs," Liza said. "Be ready."

"I'll be ready," Willem said, "ready to save your boyfriend when he gets in too deep."

"You're being childish, Willem," Liza said, "and I'm sure our leader wouldn't find that an admirable trait in his general, would he?"

"Go ahead, go!" Willem shouted. "Don't you worry about what our leader wants and doesn't want. I have the leader's ear, remember that."

"I remember," Liza said, and even she found it odd that their leader, the person they were all fighting for, would talk only to Willem and to no other man.

It was unsettling for their forces not to see the man they were supporting.

Perhaps Nick Carter would be able to do something

111

to help them. Maybe he had worked out a plan and wanted to let her know. Or maybe he just wanted to see her as much as she wanted to see him, for reasons other than just a political cause.

She had felt a strong attraction to him from the moment they met and had fought it by being sharp with him, but later she admitted her feelings to herself and was much happier after that.

If she could only find out if Carter had similar feelings, she'd be even happier.

"Let's go, Ollie," she told the young bellboy. "Let's find out what 'Mr. Taylor's' problem is."

She followed Ollie out, aware that Willem was staring hard at her back. Willem might get to be a problem with his jealousy; she just hoped that it would not end up clouding his judgment.

When Liza stepped off the elevator she was alone. Leo Valniev watched her walk to the door of Carter's room, and he hoped that his patience was about to be rewarded. She was quite lovely, he noticed as she knocked on the door; Carter was certainly doing very well for himself where women were concerned.

He also wondered how Carter was doing otherwise.

When Carter opened the door he was relieved to find Liza standing there alone, without Willem and especially without Ollie.

"Good," he said. He grabbed her by the arm before she could say anything and pulled her inside.

She was about to speak, but her eyes fell on the body

lying in a pool of drying blood on the rug and her words caught in her throat.

"As you can see," he said, following her line of sight, "I have a small problem."

"You killed him?"

"It was either kill him or have him kill me," he replied. "Which would you have preferred?"

She looked at him, her face still reflecting the shock she felt, but then she shook it off and said, "Don't be silly."

"Well, now that you agree with me, you can see what my problem is."

"What?"

"I have to get rid of him," Carter said.

"Oh, of course," she said slowly. "How?"

"I was hoping your friend Willem would have some ideas," Carter said. "Do you think he could do it without raising any kind of an alarm?"

"I don't know," she mumbled.

"Liza," Carter said, grabbing her by the arm again, "are you all right?" He was beginning to think he'd made a mistake in sending for her. Maybe he should have sent for Willem instead.

"I'm fine, I'm fine," she insisted, brushing his hand away. "Just give me a moment to think."

She started to walk away from him, but when she realized she was going in the direction of the body she abruptly changed her direction and walked past Carter to the window.

"Willem can't come into the city," she said, half aloud and half to herself. "It's too risky."

"Don't you have some people here in the city who could handle this?" Carter asked.

"I think we do," she said thoughtfully. She turned to face him. "Yes, I think we do," she said, again, her voice stronger.

"Good," Carter said. "Get them."

"It shouldn't take me too long to get in touch with them," she said, heading for the door.

"Fine—just do me one favor," Carter said.

"What?"

"Keep Ollie away from here," he said. "That boy is anything but discreet."

"Ollie's all right," she said.

"I'm sure he means well, but I'd just feel better if he didn't know about this. Okay?"

"Okay," she agreed. "We can do it without him, I'm sure."

"Good."

"Nick," she said hesitantly.

"Yes?"

"I'm sorry I froze for a moment—"

"Don't worry about it," Carter said. "Just see what you can do about getting this guy out of here. He's playing havoc with my social life."

"All right," she said.

"And see what you can do about getting somebody to clean up the blood."

"Clean it up?"

"At least enough so that the maid won't see it right away," Carter said. "If we can wash some of it out, maybe we can cover it with something and it won't be noticeable. I don't want the authorities coming around asking me questions. I don't want Mahbee to have an excuse to lock me up somewhere.''

"Mahbee!" she said, suddenly alarmed. "Mahbee must know who your are—''

"Liza," Carter said patiently, "we'll discuss that later, okay? Right now I just want you to get your people here to clean up this mess. Okay?''

"Okay," she said, but she couldn't help thinking, as she went out the door, what good Nick Carter was going to be able to do if Mahbee knew who he was.

Could Willem be right?

Could it be that this handsome American agent would be of no help to them at all?

It was hours later when Liza returned, and even the patience of Leo Valniev had begun to wear thin.

When Liza came out of the elevator this time, Valniev perked up in the stairwell. The lovely dark-haired girl had two men with her, and between them they were wheeling what appeared to be a laundry cart.

Finally he'd find out what was going on. It was too bad he had not yet had the opportunity to bug Carter's room, but this would turn out to be just as good.

"Wheel it in here," Liza instructed the two men after Carter had opened the door, and they pushed the laundry cart inside and shut the door behind them.

"Over there, fellas," Carter said, pointing, "and don't worry about the starch. I've taken it all out of him."

If the two men understood him, they gave no indication. They pushed the cart toward the dead man, removed a couple of sheets, and proceeded to wrap the man in them. That done, they each grabbed one end of the bundle, and, straining, they managed to lift the massive bulk and dump the body into the cart.

"What about the blood?" Carter asked.

One of the men reached into the cart and came out with sponges, a brush, and a container of rug cleaner.

"Just put them down," Liza said. "I'll take care of it."

The man obeyed, and then he and his partner wheeled the cart toward the door, using considerably more effort than they had used to wheel it in. Liza stepped to the door, opened it, and after they stepped out into the hallway, she spoke to one of them briefly in a low voice and then closed the door.

"They'll drive it away from here in their van and dispose of it somewhere."

"Good."

"I'll try and take care of the blood," she said.

"Let's both do it."

Between them, using water, the rug cleaner, and a lot of muscle, they managed to get out most of the blood. When they were done there was a pinkish stain on the hotel rug, and Carter decided to move the armchair to cover it, hoping the maid wouldn't feel it her duty to move the chair back to where the hotel had originally positioned it.

"How's that?" Carter asked.

"Terrific," Liza said. "I want to wash my hands."

When she finished and came back into the room,

Carter said, "There's some bourbon over there. Pour yourself a drink while I clean up."

When he came out of the bathroom he saw Liza taking a swig of bourbon straight from the bottle, and it wasn't her first. Already her face was flushed.

"Take it easy on that stuff," he advised.

"I'm all right."

"Sure you are," he agreed.

He sat next to her on the couch, took the bottle, and took a deep swallow of his own, mainly to keep her from drinking too much more of it.

"Let's talk about Mahbee," Liza said. "I'll have to report back to Willem."

Carter explained to Liza how he and Valniev had talked things over, and how Valniev had probably told Mahbee about his being on the island.

"You talked with the Russian?"

"Why not?" It's better than shooting at each other."

"I suppose, but I don't think Willem would understand it."

"Has Willem talked to your, uh, leader about me?" Carter asked.

"I don't know," Liza replied. "I know he's spoken to him since you arrived, but I don't know if they've talked about you."

"Liza, you have no idea who this mysterious leader is? No idea at all?"

"None."

"I did some reading in the library today."

"About what?"

"About the assassination of President Makumbo."

"Oh."

"Jules Berbick was never found, according to what I read."

"That's right," she said. "He's probably dead."

"Why do you say that?"

"That's what Willem keeps saying."

"He does, huh?" Carter said. "That's very interesting."

"Why?"

"What do you think of the possibility that this mystery man you're fighting to make president is Jules Berbick?"

"Impossible," she said emphatically, shaking her head.

"Why?"

"Berbick didn't do anything. He was just a figurehead, Nick."

"Was he loyal to Makumbo?"

She thought that over for a moment.

"I didn't know the man," she said finally, "but I suppose he was loyal."

"Who found the presidential limo after the assassination?"

"I don't know," she said. "Didn't it say that in the papers?"

"No. They simply said that when the limo was found, Makumbo was dead, Berbick was gone, and Mahbee and the driver were unconscious."

He took a swig from the bottle and then passed it back to her with a mouthful left.

"Suppose Berbick was only wounded and got away.

Suppose he's the man Willem has his meetings with.''

"Why wouldn't Willem tell us?"

"It serves his side's purpose better to keep insisting that Berbick is dead. If they knew he was alive, Mahbee could try to kill him—again—eliminating his competition. Besides, think how much sentiment will be on Berbick's side when he finally does appear.'' Carter looked up at the ceiling and said, " 'Wounded with his president, Jules Berbick returns to take up where President Makumbo left off.' ''

"It does make sense the way you say it," she admitted. She tilted the bottle and finished the last of the bourbon. "Maybe I should ask Willem straight out.''

"No, don't do that," Carter said. "He'd just deny it.''

She nodded and said, "Out of loyalty.''

"Or something else.''

"What do you mean?''

"I don't feel right about Willem, Liza," he said. "It's not something I can explain.''

"Willem is loyal, Nick.''

"But to whom?'' Carter asked.

"No," Liza said, shaking her head, "you're wrong about Willem, Nick.''

"All right," Carter said, "let's forget it.''

He frowned and looked around the room.

"What's wrong?''

"You know, while I was waiting for you I decided to search my room and determine whether or not it had been bugged.''

"And?''

"And it hasn't," he said. "If Valniev had wanted to

bug the room, he probably would have had to get the supplies from Mahbee."

"So?"

"So maybe he hasn't told Mahbee about me," Carter said. "Maybe that's why he didn't bug my room. Leo Valniev is a very unpredictable man, Liza. For his own reasons, he could be keeping my presence to himself."

"Now that theory I think I can blow out of the water," she said, focusing her eyes unsteadily on his.

"Oh, really?"

"Really," she said.

Carter waited, and when she didn't offer he said, "Well, go ahead. I'm all ears."

"Not all ears," she said, touching his mouth with her hand. Suddenly she leaned in close, all hungry eyes and mouth. She chewed on his lower lip for a few moments, and when she drew back she pointed to the pink spot under the armchair.

"That was Makumbo's driver, Nick," she said.

"The one who was supposedly found unconscious in the limo?" he asked.

"That's right," she said. "Him and Mahbee, and you know what his job was after that?"

"What?"

"Assistant and bodyguard to one George Mahbee."

"Mahbee's bodyguard tried to kill me?"

"That's the way it looks," she said. "Guess he knows you're here, huh?" she asked, and then she went to sleep in his arms.

When Leo Valniev saw the two men come back out

wheeling a considerably heavier laundry cart than they wheeled in, he hurried down the stairs and got to the lobby before they did. They made a detour to go out the freight entrance, and he followed. He watched them load the cart into the back of a van with CARIBE CLEANING written on the side. As they loaded it in, the edge of a sheet flapped over the side of the cart, and Valniev could see that the fabric was soaked a bright red—and he knew blood when he saw it.

He'd spilled enough of it in the past twenty years.

Leo Valniev decided it was time to have another talk with George Mahbee.

When Valniev walked into Mahbee's office he noticed that Mahbee's huge assistant was not in evidence.

"Where's your mountain?" he asked.

"Duncan?" Mahbee asked. "I sent him on an errand."

"Have you heard from him since?"

Mahbee frowned at Valniev. "No."

Valniev sat down in front of Mahbee's desk and lit a cigarette. Through a haze of smoke he stared at Mahbee and said, "I told you Nick Carter would eat your boy for lunch, Mahbee."

"What are you talkng about?"

"Your assistant got taken to the cleaners—permanently," Valniev told him. When Mahbee frowned, Valniev explained, "I'm sorry. I've seen too many American gangster films, and sometimes I talk like I'm in one." He leaned forward and said, "You sent Duncan after Nick Carter, and now he's dead."

Mahbee stiffened and said, "I will have the man arrested."

"You can't prove he killed him."

"You are a witness."

"Not to the killing," Valniev said, "just the removal of the corpse, which I saw during routine surveillance."

"That doesn't matter," Mahbee said, "I don't need proof." He reached for his phone and said, "I'll have some of my men pick him up."

Valniev leaned forward and put his hand over the receiver before Mahbee could pick it up.

"I beg your pardon," Mahbee said, fixing the Russian with a steely-eyed stare.

"That's a good way for you to lose some more men," Valniev said. "You lost Duncan because you would not listen to me. I said I would handle Nick Carter, and I will."

"I want him out of the way!" Mahbee shouted.

"You concentrate on the others," Valniev said, "and I will concentrate on Nick Carter. He won't be a problem, I promise you."

"He had better not be," Mahbee said. "Your country wants what I've got. Just remember that."

"How can I forget?" Valniev asked, standing up. "But there's something I want even more."

"What's that?"

"I want Nick Carter, and I would advise you not to get in my way again."

Something in the Russian's eyes caused a chill to rush down Mahbee's spine and then back up again.

"Meanwhile, in your little war against the people, I

would advise you to check out a business called Caribe Cleaners. You might find something useful.''

Mahbee watched as the Russian walked to the door and went through it, then he picked up a pencil and wrote "Caribe Cleaners" on a piece of paper. He shook off the shiver he had felt and wrote it off to a chill in the air. He also promised himself that, once he was in power and dealing with the Russians, part of his asking price would be the head of Leo Valniev.

ELEVEN

The next morning Carter found out two things he did not know about Megan. She was impatient—and jealous.

Since she hadn't heard from him since the day before, she decided to be bold and come to his room. When he answered the knock on his door with Wilhelmina in hand, her eyes widened.

"Who were you expecting?" she asked.

"Just somebody else," he said. His left hand remained on the door, keeping it partially shut.

"Aren't you going to invite me in?" she asked. "I've been worried about you."

"Nothing to worry about," he assured her.

"Can't I come in?"

"I don't think so," he said. "Why don't you let me call you later?"

"What's wrong, Nick?" she asked.

"Nothing. I just—"

125

He stopped short when he saw her look past him, and without turning around he knew what she was looking at.

"Oh, I get it," she said. "I'm sorry I broke in on your love nest, Nick."

He let her turn and go back down the hall to her room, and then he shut the door.

"I'm sorry," Liza said when he turned to face her.

"No problem," he assured her.

"I think she got the wrong idea," Liza said. She looked down at herself just then and saw that she was wearing one of the shirts from Carter's closet.

"She did get the wrong idea, didn't she?"

"You don't remember?"

"What?"

"You went to sleep after you dropped that bomb about my friend being Mahbee's assistant."

"And you put me to bed?"

"As gently as I knew how," he said. "Want some breakfast? I'll call room service."

"Are you kidding?" she asked. "I've been sleeping and eating in caves for the past week."

"Breakfast," he said. He called room service and ordered two large American-style breakfasts while Liza went into the bathroom and took a shower.

"That was wonderful," she said, coming out of the bathroom wearing one towel and drying her hair with the other. She was grinning from ear to ear.

"Leave a ring around my shower stall?" he asked.

"You can plant a garden now."

"Breakfast should be here in about fifteen minutes,'' Carter said. He was willing to bet that it would be delivered by Ollie.

It was.

As Ollie wheeled in the breakfast cart he saw Liza in her towel and his jaw dropped.

"Just leave it, Ollie," Carter said. "I'll do the serving."

For once Ollie was struck speechless. He simply nodded and backed out the door.

"He must really have been shook up," Carter said. "He didn't even wait for a tip."

"He'll tell Willem about this," she said.

"Does that bother you?"

"Only that he'll be mad for no reason at all," she said. She approached Carter, toying with the towel that was wrapped around her and added, "Or maybe we can give him a reason?"

Carter tugged at the towel and it flared and fell to the ground.

Liza stepped forward and put her arms around his neck, crushing her breasts to his chest. Her mouth closed hungrily over his, and he had no trouble at all in matching her eagerness.

"Mmm," she said, sliding her lips down over his chin to his neck while unbuttoning his shirt. When she had it open, she slid it down off his shoulders and began to kiss his chest, lingering with her tongue over his nipples.

"Liza," he said.

"Hmm?" she replied, kissing his neck once again.

"I've got too many clothes on."

"I noticed," she said. "I think we can do something about that . . ."

Later Liza told him that the cold breakfast was delicious, considering the rations she had been eating recently.

"The rest was warm enough, though," she added happily, smiling at him across the breakfast table. He smiled back.

"Uh, that girl . . . at the door . . ."

"She works with me," Carter said. "She was vacationing here when the island got sealed off."

"You didn't know her before?"

He shook his head.

"Just met her a couple of days ago."

That seemed to make Liza even happier, and she poured herself another cup of coffee.

"You don't seem to drink very well," he said, referring to the evening before.

"Never could," she answered, "but I was trying to blot *that* out of my mind," and she indicated the pinkish stain beneath the armchair.

"Well, I can't say that I blame you," he said, leaning forward, "but if we had talked it over, I'm sure we could have figured out a better way."

"Have you decided on how you might help us, Nick?" Liza asked.

She was dressed now, and her clothes didn't look half bad thanks to Carter, who had kept her from sleeping in them all night.

128

"I may have, Liza," he said. "I think maybe Willem and I should sit down and talk about it."

"I don't think he'll take you to the leader," she said, "if that's what you're thinking."

"I think he will," Carter said.

"What makes you so sure?"

"Because I won't go ahead with what I have in mind unless he does," Carter said. "I want to see the man I'm fighting for before I go any further."

She started to shake her head again, but he spoke before she could.

"He'll do it, Liza, because the man will tell him to. If he doesn't, he won't become president. It's that simple."

"You seem confident," she said, "and you're starting to make me believe you."

"Hey," he said, "that's a major triumph right there, isn't it?"

"Considering the way I was acting when we first met," she admitted, "yes, it is."

She stood up and said, "Thanks for everything you've done so far, Nick. Like breakfast, like last night . . . like this morning . . . just everything."

She was tall, but she still had to get on tiptoe to kiss him on the mouth.

"I'll go and talk to Willem, and arrange a meeting between the two of you. Will you be here?"

"If I'm not, give the message to Ollie. He'll see I get it—that is, if he doesn't put a knife in my back for what he saw this morning."

"He wouldn't," she assured him. "What about

your, uh, lady friend? Couldn't I leave the message with her?''

"No, I don't want to get her in any deeper than she already is," he said. "Just me or Ollie, okay?"

"Whatever you say."

He walked her to the door and checked the hallway before allowing her to leave.

"Be careful," he told her.

"I will be," she said. "I promise. And she kissed him again.

He watched her until she got in the elevator, then closed the door and went to take a shower. When he came out he got dressed and tried to figure what his next move should be. There really was not much he could do until he spoke to Willem and put his proposition to him, a proposition he didn't think the man would be able to refuse—not outright, anyway. Not without talking with "the man" first.

That was what Carter was counting on. Once Berbick—or whoever the man was—had agreed to see him, he'd put his plan into effect immediately, the only plan he'd been able to come up with.

He only hoped that what Santa Caribe had to offer was worth it.

Once again when the knock sounded on Carter's door he expected either Ollie or Megan. It was too soon for Liza to be returning from her meeting with Willem.

That it was Leo Valniev was a big, if not total, surprise.

"Leo."

"May I come in, my friend?" the Russian asked, "Or do you have someone here with you?"

"No, no, I'm alone, Leo," Carter said. "Come in."

"Thank you."

Carter closed the door behind his guest and asked, "Can I get something for you from room service? I'm afraid the coffee I have is from breakfast, and cold."

"No, no, my friend, I require nothing," Valniev said. He was looking around the room for something, and apparently something specific, but Carter couldn't figure out what it was.

A body? he thought suddenly.

He was watching the Russian's face when the man's eyes fell on the out-of-place armchair—the furnishings were arranged almost identically in each suite if Carter could judge from his and Megan's rooms—and then on the pinkish, washed-out stain beneath it.

"Find what you were looking for?" Carter asked.

Valniev looked over at him, then smiled and sat down on the couch across from the armchair.

"I understand you had some dirty laundry removed yesterday," Valniev said.

"Is that so?"

"Yes," Valniev replied. "I just wanted you to know, my friend, that I had nothing to do with it."

"I never thought you had, Leo," Carter said. "Strongarm is just not your style."

"Style," Valniev said as if savoring the word. "There is little of that left in our business these days, my friend."

"I know what you mean."

"You and I are the last of an old and stylish lot, Nick. When we are gone, the entire game will undergo a change."

"It's already changed, Leo," Carter said, "all around us. We just haven't given into it—yet."

"And we won't," Valniev said, slapping his hands on his knees and getting up. "I guarantee it."

"That remains to be seen."

"Yes, I suppose it does," Valniev said. He walked to the door, then stopped with his hand on the doorknob and said, "Oh, by the way, I'd warn that laundry service of yours, Caribe Cleaners? They may be getting some business they don't like in a little while."

"Well, thanks, Leo. That's very sporting of you."

"Don't count on it," Valniev said and left.

Carter went to the phone immediately and dialed for room service, asking for Ollie.

When the bellboy came on, Carter did not give him a chance to say anything.

"Ollie, your friends in the laundry business?"

"Uh, yes?"

"If I were you, I would advise them to move their operation . . . now!"

"Why, that—"

"Their rent is about to go sky high, and they'll never be able to survive, understand?"

"I understand," Ollie said, for once quick on the uptake.

"Good," Carter said and hung up.

Somehow Valniev knew about the entire incident, including the method of disposal. No doubt he had reported to Mahbee, but why turn around and warn Carter that the "cleaners" was going to be hit?

As in the past, Leo Valniev was proving to be unpredictable—and maybe that was the only reason he did it.

It proved very difficult for Liza to talk Willem into a meeting with Nick Carter.

"Did you have a pleasant night?" he asked snidely. "We did not expect you to be gone the entire night."

"I didn't expect to either, but that's the way it happened," she said, "and I have no intention of explaining myself to you."

Willem grabbed Liza's arm, but he let it go almost immediately.

"Nick has an idea of how he can help, but he wants to have a meeting with—"

"I know who he wants to meet with!" Willem snapped. He turned and walked away from her a few steps, then turned back.

"It's impossible!"

Liza reacted with a shocked look.

"That's not for you to decide," she said.

He stared at her grimly for a long moment, as if at a loss for words, and then said, "You're right. Wait here, and I will talk to—to our leader."

Willem left the cave where they had first brought Nick Carter and, traveling alone, went to speak with his wounded leader.

When he returned, Liza could see by the look on his face that he was not pleased.

"Well?"

He glared at her with fiery eyes, and for the first time in her life she was a little afraid of him. She actually backed away from his glare, one hand at her throat.

"You tell your friend, Nick Carter, that he will have his meeting," he told her, "but I want you to know, Liza, that I argued against this. It can only lead to disaster. Our leader is safe as long as no one knows where he is. You will have helped expose him to danger."

"Nick Carter is no danger to us or our leader," Liza said, "and you know it, Willem. Sometimes I think your jealousy—"

"Jealousy?" Willem screeched. "Of you?"

"No, your jealousy concerning your relationship with the man you always call 'our leader' doesn't let you see things clearly," she shot back.

Suddenly Willem seemed to become quite calm, and the look in his eyes seemed to soften.

"Deliver the message to Carter, Liza, and bring him here to me," he said quietly, and for some reason the soft tone of his voice frightened her even more than his fiery gaze had moments before.

Carter was waiting in his room when Liza called and said she was coming up. She would not say on the phone whether or not the meeting had been arranged. When he let her in, however, she came right to the point.

"You've got your meeting, Nick."

"When?"

"I'm to take you to Willem now."

"And he'll take me to your leader?" Carter asked, realizing he sounded like something out of a grade B science fiction movie.

"That's what he said."

"Do you believe him?"

"Why would he lie, Nick?" she asked. "I told you, Willem is loyal."

Somehow she did not sound quite as positive as she had previously sounded, Carter thought.

"All right," he said, "but we've got one stop to make first."

"Where?"

"Down the hall."

"Your . . . partner?"

"Yes," he said. He grabbed his jacket and put it on over his shoulder holster.

"You're going to bring your gun?"

"Leaving it here would be like leaving my arm behind," Carter told her.

She looked dubious but did not argue the point.

Liza followed Carter out of the room and down the hall. He knocked on Megan's door, hoping she was there.

When Megan opened the door, it was obvious that she did not like or approve of what she saw.

"Don't tell me you ran out of things to do down the hall?" she asked them.

"Stop being childish, Megan," Carter said. He walked through the doorway, forcing Megan to step back, and Liza followed close behind him, keeping quiet.

"What do you want?"

"I want you to act like an adult and listen," Carter told her. "This is Liza. She's taking me into the hills to meet with the leader of the Makumbo faction. If I don't come back, Megan, it will be up to you to make some kind of a report to Washington. Do you understand that?"

"If . . . if you don't come back?" she asked. "Do you mean to tell me that you're going with this woman into the hills alone? That's crazy, Nick! You need some kind of a backup—"

"Who would you suggest?" he interrupted her.

"Well . . . I could—"

"Look, honey," he said, taking her by the shoulders, "it's a nice thought, but I need you to stay behind for the reason I just gave. Do that for me, all right?"

"How long—how long should I—"

"If you don't hear from me by tomorrow, figure I'm not coming back," he told her.

"Nick—"

"Just wish me luck, Megan."

She hesitated a moment, looking at Liza, then threw her arms around Carter and hugged him, saying, "Come back, Nick. Good luck."

"I'll see you tomorrow," he told her. He turned to Liza and said, "Let's go."

Liza pushed away from the wall where she had been leaning and followed Carter out into the hall.

"Your friend Megan seems concerned," she commented to him in the elevator.

"I hope she is," Carter said, "and I hope you are, too."

"Are you?"

"Very," he said. "I told you, I don't quite trust Willem's motives in this—and I don't want to discuss this with you right now. Just take me to him."

TWELVE

The trek through the hills was reminiscent of the one they had made following their first meeting, except for one thing.

That time, no one had taken a shot at them.

At the sound of the shot, Carter grabbed Liza and pulled her to the ground, keeping himself on top of her.

"Are you all right?" he asked.

"Yes," she answered breathlessly. "I just lost a little of my wind. What happened?"

"Somebody took a shot at us," he said. He lifted his head to look around, but he couldn't see anything. They had fallen together between some large rocks, and Carter was sure they were no longer visible.

"Just stay down," he told her, sliding his weight from her.

"What are you going to do?"

"We'll wait a few moments, and then I'll have to see if whoever fired that shot is still out there."

"Who do you think it was?" she asked. "The Russian?"

"No," he said, "not the Russian."

He looked at Liza, and it was as if she were able to read his mind.

"You can't think it's Willem!"

"Is Willem a decent shot?"

"He's an excellent shot," she maintained. "If he had fired that shot, he would have hit you."

"If that's what he wanted to do," Carter added.

Looking exasperated she asked, "Why would he shoot at you if he didn't want to hit you?"

"I can't answer that, Liza," he said, "not yet. Stay put—I'm going to check."

As he lifted his head up, there was another shot, and a slug of lead struck the rock very close to his face, sending slivers into his cheek. He recoiled, falling back next to Liza and putting his hand over his cheek.

"Let me see!" Liza cried.

"It's nothing," he said. but he dropped his hand so she could look at it.

"It's not bad," she said. "A piece of rock opened a cut."

"He's still out there," Carter said.

"What about your gun?"

"He's using a rifle. My Luger isn't any good at this range. We'll have to think of a way out of here."

"We can cut down this way," Liza said, "between the rocks. It'll take us close to the base of the hill. If he's on top, he won't be able to see us."

"All right," Carter said, glad she knew the terrain, "lead the way."

He followed her along a path through the rocks, and soon they were going down the hill instead of up.

"How far out of the way will this take us?" he asked.

"It's not so much that it will take us out of the way; it'll just take us a bit longer to get there."

"As long as we get there," Carter said, "and in one piece."

As they continued to walk, keeping to the base of the hill, there were no further shots.

"What if he's waiting for us on the other side?" Liza asked.

"I don't think he will be," Carter said. "For all he knows, we're looking for a way to get up the hill, and my guess is he's on his way down right now. He had his two shots and he missed. I'm going to make that meeting after all."

"You still think it was Willem," she said. "You think he just wanted to prevent you from keeping this meeting, right?"

"Who knew about it, Liza, besides you and Willem?"

"Your girl friend, in the hotel."

"She wouldn't have had the time to set it up even if she wanted to," he answered. "Willem's the best bet for this."

"So why don't you ask him when you see him?" she asked.

"I will," he said, "but after my meeting with the big man, the next president of Santa Caribe. It's Jules Berbick, isn't it, Liza?"

She turned around to face him and said, "I honestly

don't know. How many times do I have to tell you?''

"It's not how many times you've been telling me, Liza," he said, "it's how hard. Too hard."

"We're almost there," she said angrily, turning her back on him. "Come on."

He followed her the rest of the way in silence, and when they got around the hill, there was nobody waiting to shoot them.

As they approached the cave, Carter recognized the terrain.

"Same place as before?"

"Yes," she said, "but you wouldn't have been able to find it from the city."

"I know," he admitted.

As she began to clear away the brush from the entrance, Carter caught a whiff of a smell that made him grab her arm and pull her back. With his other hand he drew Wilhelmina from under his jacket.

"What's wrong?"

"I smell something," he said. There had been some shooting in that cave very recently. The sharp odor of cordite filled his nostrils as he stepped through the entrance.

"Stay behind me," he warned her, and she did, very close behind him. She rode his back like a second skin.

There were four men in the cave, and they were all dead. He knew that even before he went to each man, turned him over, and examined the body.

"Is—are any of them—" she stammered.

"Willem's not here," he said, turning to face her.

Her sense of relief changed to feelings of fear very quickly as she realized what that might mean to Carter.

142

"Oh, Nick, no—"

"I didn't say a thing."

"But you were thinking it."

"Do you know any of these men?"

She looked down at the four men, at their empty faces.

"Yes, I do," she said.

"Then mourn for them," Carter said, "and feel sorry for their families if they had any. Let me worry about Willem."

Carter holstered his gun and wondered how he was going to have that meeting.

"Come on," Liza said suddenly.

"Where to?" he asked. "The meeting's a bust now, and I don't think Willem's going to come back here."

"I'll take you to see . . . to see the leader," she said.

"You'll take me?"

She nodded, looking solemn.

"Liza—"

"I know," she said, "I lied to you, but I had to—but I don't have to anymore. Come on, I'll take you to him."

"But how do you know where he is?" he asked. "Why do you know?"

"That's simple," she said. "I know because he's my father."

Carter followed Liza through the brush in stunned silence. There was nothing else to be said, at least not until they got to where they were going.

So the man they were trying to put into the Presidential Building was Liza's father—but was he Jules Berbick? He'd find that out soon enough.

And what was Willem's story? Was he a plant all along, working for Mahbee? If so, why hadn't he already killed Liza's father?

There were so many questions, more questions than there were answers, probably, but the answers—some of them—would be known soon enough.

That is, if somebody hadn't got there ahead of them.

"Another cave?" Carter asked when they stopped in a small valley between several hills.

"Not really," she said. Instead of approaching one of the surrounding hills, Liza led Carter toward the center of the valley, and suddenly the ground beneath them changed.

"Wood," he said, banging his foot.

"There's a mine shaft beneath us," she said. "That's where he is."

Liza put her back against a broad-based tree, then marked off a number of paces. That done, she bent over, brushed away some dirt and leaves, then slid her finger into a metal ring. Tugging, she began to struggle with a heavy wooden door, and Carter stepped forward to help her get it open.

"Let me go first," Carter cautioned her, taking out his gun.

She hesitated, concern for her father threatening to overcome caution, but finally she stepped back and allowed him to descend first.

When they got to the bottom of the shaft she said, "We should close the door behind us."

He looked up and agreed, and proceeded to go back up to shut the door. It was too heavy for her to do it. She waited for him to close it and come back, and then he started off down the shaft ahead of her.

"Is your father armed?" he asked.

"He has a handgun, yes," she said.

Ahead of them he saw part of a lighted area, and she said, "That's it ahead."

"Slow down," he said, holding a hand out behind him. He flattened himself against the side of the shaft and moved cautiously toward the lighted area, holding Wilhelmina next to his face.

When he reached the entrance to the lighted shaft, he peered in and saw a man lying on a cot, a swathe of bloodstained bandages around his chest. He could not tell whether or not the man was breathing. There did not appear to be anyone else in the room.

"What's happening?" she asked, coming up behind him.

"Looks empty," he said.

Liza looked past Carter at her father, and she too could not tell if he was breathing.

"Father," she cried, and ran across the room.

"Liza—" Carter called, but she was beyond caution. He moved in behind her, keeping his eyes open and his gun ready.

"Father," she said again, kneeling next to the man on the cot. She touched his shoulder, and for a moment he did not react and she feared the worst, then. . . .

The man groaned and turned over slowly to face his daughter. Carter recognized him from pictures he had seen in the library.

"Father," Liza breathed in relief.

"Jules Berbick," Carter said, and the man looked past his daughter at Carter and grabbed for the gun on the cot next to him.

"It's all right," she told him, laying her hand over the gun. "He's Nick Carter."

"The American?"

"Yes."

"Help me to sit up," Berbick told his daughter, struggling to get his arms beneath him to push himself up.

"Easy," she cautioned him. When he was sitting up, she piled a couple of pillows behind him.

Berbick had been sleeping when they arrived, and gradually he seemed to be coming awake. His eyes were cloudy at first, but they were clear now—except for when they glazed over with pain.

"Father, Nick guessed that you were alive," Liza explained.

"I see," Berbick said. "Why did you bring him here, and not Willem?"

Liza looked up at Carter, and Carter said, "Willem has disappeared, Mr. Berbick, and four of his men are dead."

"Dead?" Berbick asked. "Mahbee's soldiers?"

"We don't know," Carter replied. "We won't know until we can find Willem and ask him what happened."

Carter looked around, found a couple of chairs, and pulled them over so both he and Liza could sit.

"What I'd like to know now is what happened to

you, Mr. Vice-President.''

"It was Mahbee," Berbick said. "He shot Makumbo, and then he turned the gun on me. I was reacting right away, out of panic. I was going out the door when he shot me, and the bullet entered on the right side of my chest.''

Berbick touched his bandaged chest to show Carter where he was wounded.

"I kept running into the brush and hid," Berbick said. "After they gave up looking for me I went to Willem, and he hid me.''

"Just who is Willem?" Carter asked.

Berbick hesitated a moment, then said, "Willem is one of our younger men who has always been loyal to Santa Caribe, and to me.''

Carter waited for Berbick to continue, and when he didn't, he said, "There's more."

"Yes," Berbick said. "Willem is—was—Bili Makumbo's son.''

"I see," Carter said. That explained the man's loyalty better than anything else could have.

"Mahbee thinks that having been Makumbo's bodyguard, and being injured himself while trying to protect his president, will win him the election as President Makumbo's replacement.''

"So you let the word out that there was someone who was going to run against him, but you did not say who.''

"Correct."

"And when you appear, wounded but alive, you hope that sentiment will be on your side.''

"Yes."

"And when will you appear?"

"When he's well enough," Liza answered.

"Has he had proper medical treatment?" Carter asked.

"One of our people had some training," she said.

"Well, where is he?'

"Right now he's lying in that cave back there, dead," Liza said.

"So you've never been treated here by a doctor?"

"No."

"May I look at your wound?" Carter asked.

"Of course."

Liza backed away so that Carter could get in close and unwind the bandages to take a look.

"Was the bullet removed?" he asked.

"Yes," Berbick said.

"That's lucky," Carter remarked. With the bandage off he examined the wound, and it seemed clean enough. There were no telltale signs of infection, but it did not seem to be healing quickly.

Rebandaging the wound Carter said, "Your medic seems to have known what he was doing, but it will still be some time before you are ready to put in a personal appearance."

"Mahbee has been cooperating with us so far," Berbick said.

"How do you mean?"

"Mahbee has control over the elections and when they will be held," Berbick explained. "Instead of scheduling it and forcing me out in the open, he seems to want to find me first, and that is giving me time to recover."

Carter agreed. The thing for Mahbee to do was to schedule the elections and get it over with, and as soon as Valniev realized that fact, he would make the suggestion.

He finished rewinding the bandage, having made it considerably tighter than it was, and returned to his chair.

"What were the plans for taking you to the city?" Carter asked. "You're certainly in no shape to hoof it."

"I beg your pardon?"

"You're in no shape to walk," Liza said, translating.

"No," Berbick said, "you are quite right. Willem was going to get a vehicle to drive me into the city."

"Well, we'll have to take care of that, then," Carter said.

"Father, did Willem ask you about meeting with Nick?" Liza asked.

"Yes, he did. He said that Mr. Carter had a plan, but that he would not reveal it unless he met and spoke to me." Berbick looked at Carter and said, "And now you are here."

"Yes, and I'm very curious about something," Carter said.

"What?"

"Your reputation," Carter said, "as a do-nothing, figurehead vice-president."

The man on the cot did not strike Carter as that sort

of man. For him to be talking about traveling to the city and fighting for the presidency while recovering from a serious bullet wound, Berbick was showing a lot of courage and determination. That did not fit the image of the man Carter had read about.

"A carefully constructed reputation, Mr. Carter," Jules Berbick answered.

Carter caught on immediately.

"So then it was Bili Makumbo who was the figurehead—and you were making all of the decisions behind the scenes."

"Correct," Berbick said, "against the eventuality that something like this would happen. Bili didn't mind. He was devoted to me, and to Santa Caribe."

"And Mahbee almost got you both," Carter said. "How did you allow yourself and Makumbo to be caught together so easily?"

"It was George Mahbee," Berbick said. "Bili allowed himself to be convinced that it was the best way for us to travel to the park that day."

"It was sheer luck that you got away, then."

"Yes," he said, "luck and panic, which gave wings to my feet."

"That's nothing to be ashamed of, sir, believe me," Carter assured him.

"I'm not, Mr. Carter," Berbick replied, "I'm not. Tell me, what is this plan you've come up with?"

"It is a very simple one."

"And that is?"

Carter looked at Liza, then back at her father and said, very simply, "Kill Mahbee."

"Assassinate him?" Berbick asked after a moment of stunned silence.

"That's what started all of this, isn't it?" Carter said.

"Well, yes, but—"

"But you don't want to sink to his level."

The look on Berbick's face told Carter that he was right on target, although Berbick couldn't think of how to put it into words.

"If he's going to fight dirty, sir, then you're going to have to play dirty to win."

"But who would do it?" Berbick asked.

"I would."

Berbick looked closely at Carter's face and said, "You do not strike me as a man who is an assassin for hire, Mr. Carter."

"I'm not," Carter said, "but I will do whatever I have to do to get the job done. I don't see any way around this."

"There must be another way."

"Then show it to me," Carter said. "His forces outnumber yours by a wide margin. It's only a matter of time before he finds you . . . and we don't know what Willem has up his sleeve."

"What do you mean?"

"Nick doesn't trust Willem, Father," Liza said.

"Why not?"

"What did you promise Willem, Mr. Vice-President?"

"A position in my administration."

"Did he let you know what position he would like?"

"Of course," Berbick said. "He would like to be vice-president, but I explained that he was much too young for such a position."

"I'll bet he didn't like that."

"Perhaps not," Berbick said, "but he understood."

"Maybe he did, and maybe he didn't," Carter said. "He's young and ambitious, and if he could get more from Mahbee, maybe he'd go that way."

"I can't believe that—"

"Then where is he?" Carter asked. "Why didn't he meet me to bring me here, and why isn't he dead in that cave with those other men?"

"There could be other explanations," Berbick said.

"Maybe so, but if we have to go on with Willem, I think we have to watch him very carefully."

"What do you propose?"

"We set up a meeting between you and Mahbee, only I'll be the one to meet him."

"How do you know he'll come?"

"He wants to meet the man who is his only opposition," Carter said, "but to make sure he comes, we'll tell him that it's you, that you're alive, and that you want to see him. Did he have any idea that you were the power behind the presidency?"

"I don't know," Berbick said slowly. "He's very clever, but he dealt mostly with Bili, who was himself starting to take the position seriously."

"We'll have to get a message to Mahbee," Carter said. "I can handle that through the Russian, Leo Valniev."

"What do you want me to do?" Liza asked.

"You'll have to explain to me how to get back to the city from here," he said, although he was reasonably sure he could find his way back.

"I'm not coming with you?"

"I want you to stay here with your father until I get back," Carter said.

"What about the meeting with Mahbee?" she asked. "How will we get my father there?"

"I thought I explained that," Carter said. "The only one meeting with Mahbee will be me. You and your father will stay here until Mahbee is dead. At that time, Mr. Vice-President, you can step forward and take over."

"I still wish there was another way," Berbick said sadly.

"Believe me," Carter said, standing up, "so do I."

Carter started back to Caribe City not feeling particularly satisfied with himself or with his plan. What he'd said to Berbick had been true: he was not an assassin for hire. He had killed in the past, but not for the sake of killing. Here he had decided that the best way to get the job done was to take Mahbee out of the picture. If he could think of another way to do it between now and when he met with Mahbee, then he would go ahead with a new plan. But until he did that, he had to concentrate on killing George Mahbee and then getting the hell off Santa Caribe without being discovered.

If he killed Mahbee and got away without being found out, Hawk would be satisfied; but if he killed him and it got out that an American agent had done it, he would be finished with Hawk and AXE, and with the United States.

Was the cardium that important to the U.S.?

The answer was simple. He wouldn't have been sent in if it wasn't.

THIRTEEN

By the time Carter got back to Caribe City it was dark, and he had to be careful of the soldiers who were patrolling, enforcing the curfew. He did not relax at all until he was in his hotel room, standing beneath a stinging hot shower spray, and even then Wilhelmina was on the counter within easy reach.

When he got out of the shower he slowly and carefully searched his room, once again looking for listening devices and once again coming up empty. Following that, he called Megan Ward to advise her that he was back.

"Can I come over, Nick?"

"Sure, Megan. Come on over," he told her.

It took her only a few seconds to rush down the hall and knock on his door, and then she was in his arms, hugging him tightly.

"I'm glad you're back," she said.

"So am I," he answered, drawing her into the room and shutting the door.

"I want to apologize for my attitude and behavior—"

"Forget it," he said. "Have you eaten?"

"No."

"I'm starved," he said. "I'll call room service, and we'll have dinner here, okay?"

"Fine."

After he had made the call she asked him to tell her what had happened. He explained that he had met with the leader of the Makumbo people, had discussed the situation with him, and had made a decision on how to proceed.

"What are you going to do?"

"I'm going to take care of it so I can go home and you can get on with your vacation," he answered.

"No, I mean what *exactly* are you going to do?"

"Well, right now I'm going to get dressed before room service shows up with dinner," he said. "Excuse me."

Carter didn't want to tell Megan any more than she absolutely had to know, and she certainly didn't have to know that he was planning to assassinate George Mahbee.

When there was a knock on the door, she called out, "I'll get it. It must be room service."

"No!" Carter yelled out from the bedroom. He grabbed the Luger and ran into the other room clad only in his underwear, holding the gun out in front of him. Both Megan and the bellboy stared at him with shocked looks on their faces, and he executed a neat hundred-and-eighty-degree turn and went back into the bedroom.

When he came out fully clothed he asked Megan, "What did you tell the bellboy?"

"I told him you were a mystery writer and that you got very involved in your plots. You also owe me ten dollars."

"Tip?"

"Bribe," she said. "We don't want him spreading stories about the crazy American who runs around almost nude waving a gun, do we?"

"No, we don't," he agreed with a laugh.

During dinner she said, "You're not going to tell me what your plan is, are you?"

"Nope."

"Why not?"

"I don't want you involved," he said. "If it backfires, I want to be the only one who gets caught in the aftermath."

"That's not fair to you."

"It's the way it works, Megan."

"It stinks," she said, but she didn't argue further—except for one more question. "Nick, it couldn't be that you don't trust me, could it?"

Carter stared at her and asked, "Why would you even ask me that, Megan? Is there some reason why I shouldn't trust you?"

"None that I know of," she said, "but I thought that was an occupational hazard of your business, not trusting people."

"It is," he agreed, "but I don't see any reason not to trust you. By the same token, I also don't see any reason why I should involve you any deeper than necessary. Fair?"

She nodded. "Fair."

After dinner they moved to the couch with cups of coffee and brandies, and Carter relaxed for the first time that day.

"It's been rough on you, hasn't it?" she asked.

"That's nothing new," he said, sipping his coffee.

"Tell me, Nick, when do you ever get a chance to relax?"

"Once in a while," he said, "when the fate of the civilized world doesn't hang in the balance."

"You're joking."

"Of course."

She studied him for a few moments, then said, "No, maybe you're not joking."

"I'm joking, Megan."

"What are your plans for the rest of the night?"

"Since you're so concerned about my relaxing," he said, "maybe I'll just sit back tonight and relax."

She put her coffee cup down and moved closer to him on the couch.

"Do you mind if I volunteer to help you relax?" she asked.

"No, I don't mind at all," he said, putting his own cup down.

She slid her hand between two buttons on his shirt and opened them, then slid her hand all the way in and began to make circles on his chest with her palm.

"Lie down on your stomach," she whispered, "and I'll give you a massage."

"A massage?"

"I'm very good at massages," she said.

"Well, maybe it would be easier if I lay down on my stomach . . . on the bed."

"Good idea," she said.

They got up and walked to the bedroom, where she helped Carter off with his shirt.

"That feels good," he said as she began kneading the muscles in his back.

She kept it up a bit longer. "I know how to make it feel even better," she purred.

Her hands disappeared, Carter heard the rustle of clothing and then she was back, lightly moving her bare breasts up and down his spine just touching his skin with her hardened nipples.

"Now I'm really going to help you relax, Nick," she whispered into his ear. He didn't protest as she turned him over, and he even helped her a bit as she removed the rest of his clothes.

The following morning, Megan left Carter's room and headed back to hers. She had wanted to have breakfast with him, but Carter vetoed the idea; he didn't want her to be seen in public with him anymore.

"I meant up here," she'd said.

"I have to go out, Megan," had been his cryptic answer. "Early."

So, feeling disappointed and a little worried, she went back to her own room while he showered, dressed, and soon left his.

Carter needed two things. Number one, he needed a message taken to George Mahbee, ostensibly from Jules Berbick, asking Mahbee to meet him. Second, he needed someplace to have the meeting, someplace isolated, and he had to find it without anyone's help, especially not Ollie's.

Actually, except for Ollie, there was no one he could have asked for help: Willem was still missing; Liza was with her father; and Carter didn't know any other island residents. He was going to have to find the place himself, and that meant taking the morning to look over the city.

He could have used either the docks or the airstrip by simply putting in the message that Mahbee was to take the guards off either place and meet Berbick there alone, but Carter doubted that Mahbee would follow those instructions to the letter.

In fact, he doubted very much if Mahbee would follow any instructions to the letter. Maybe the trick was to figure on that.

It was early afternoon before Carter remembered the cul-de-sac he had tried to lead Mahbee's man, Duncan, into. It could be the ideal place.

He found it again, went in through the alley, and checked it out. There were a couple of other possible exits aside from the alley leading in, and that made it perfect. In the event of a foul-up, he would have an escape route. In fact, even if everything went as planned, he'd need an escape route.

He had no intention of killing Mahbee and hanging around.

The message was the easy part.

Carter was walking through the lobby, planning on going up to the fifth floor to Leo Valniev's room, but just at that moment he spotted Valniev going into the dining room to have a late lunch, so he made a detour.

"Leo," he said, walking to the Russian's table.

"Ah, my friend Nick," Valniev said. "Will you join me for lunch?"

"I'm afraid I can't," Carter said, "but I would like to talk to you for a moment."

"Please, sit," Valniev said.

"Leo, I have a message for George Mahbee."

"Really? What is the message?"

At that point the waiter came over to the table and Valniev ordered his lunch.

"And you, sir?" the waiter asked Carter.

"Nothing, thanks."

When the waiter left, Valniev said, "You were saying something about a message?"

"Yes," Carter said. "It's from Jules Berbick."

"Berbick?" Valniev asked, frowning. "Wasn't he the vice-president who was killed with Makumbo?"

"He was Makumbo's vice-president, all right, but he's far from dead."

"Are you telling me that Berbick is Mahbee's competition for the presidency?"

"That's right."

"And he has a message for Mahbee?"

"Yes," Carter replied. "He wants to meet with Mahbee. Alone. He thinks there's been too much killing."

"What does he want to talk about?" Valniev asked, looking at Carter suspiciously.

"I don't know, Leo," Carter said. "I'm just delivering the message."

"Why you?"

"Why not?" he asked. "We were both sent here to help, weren't we? I offered to deliver the message, and you can take it to Mahbee."

"I see," the Russian said. "This sounds like some kind of a trap to me."

"If that's the case, you're Mahbee's advisor. Advise him not to show up."

"I might do just that."

"Fine," Carter said, standing up. "I simply said I'd deliver the message, and I have."

"Not all of it," Valniev said. "Where does Berbick propose this meeting take place?"

Carter gave Valniev the location of the cul-de-sac and instructions on how to get there from the hotel.

"I don't know how to get there from the Presidential Building, but you might want to go there and check it out first."

"Yes, I might."

Carter stepped aside to allow the waiter to put Valniev's lunch down on the table, and then he said, "Have a good lunch, my friend."

"I intend to," the Russian said. He watched Carter's retreating back until he was out of sight, and then he leaned his elbows on the table and wondered what the American agent was up to.

"I have a message," Valniev told George Mahbee, "relayed to me by Carter."

"From who?"

"Jules Berbick."

Mahbee stared at Valniev, then laughed. "That's impossible. Berbick is dead."

"That is not my information," Valniev stated flatly.

"What is your information?"

"Jules Berbick wishes to meet with you. Alone."

"For what purpose?"

"Maybe he wants to surrender," Valniev suggested.

"Where does he want to meet?" Mahbee asked, and Valniev told him.

"Do you know where that is?" Valniev asked.

"No," Mahbee admitted, "not exactly, but it won't be hard to find."

"I've checked it out," Valniev said. "It's a cul-de-sac with one entrance and one exit, unless you want to climb a wall and go through a window."

"Berbick wouldn't be in any shape to do that," Mahbee said.

"Oh? Why not?"

"Well, I'm assuming he was injured during the assassination," Mahbee said.

The fool, Valniev thought. *Does he really think that no one knows he was the one who killed Makumbo? He probably shot Berbick as well, which is why he was so sure that the man was dead. Well, now he's got a little surprise.*

"When is this meeting supposed to take place?" Mahbee asked.

"If you tell me that you agree to meet, I will find out for you," Valniev said.

Mahbee hesitated and began tapping the top of his desk with a pencil.

"It's an opportunity to make the election a one-candidate affair," Valniev prompted him.

"I understand that," Mahbee said, "but it could also be a trap."

"That is true," the Russian said, but he offered no opinion.

"All right," Mahbee said abruptly. "Make the arrangements."

"When would you prefer?"

"Try and make it for tomorrow," Mahbee said, "In daylight."

"I doubt that would be acceptable," Valniev said.

"Well, make it for whenever Berbick wants," Mahbee said. "He's going to get more than he bargains for, anyway."

What's one more murder, give or take? Valniev thought.

Carter found a message at the desk to meet Valniev—or "Mr. Horst"—at the bar for a drink, and when he got there he found the drink already on the bar.

"Russian vodka?" Carter asked, sliding onto the bar stool.

"What else?"

"What else," Carter agreed and knocked the drink back. "I'd still rather have bourbon," he said, putting down the empty glass. "What's the occasion?"

"Your meeting has been approved."

"Not my meeting."

"No, of course not," Valniev said. "You are just delivering a message."

"Right."

"Tomorrow is all right with Mahbee," Valniev said. "Why don't you let me know when your man wants to meet, and I'll pass it along."

"Make it tomorrow night," Carter said. "Around seven."

"It gets dark about six-thirty, doesn't it?" Valniev asked.

"Leo," Carter said, getting off the stool, "you've been around long enough to know when it gets dark."

"And dangerous," the Russian said.

"Yeah," Carter said, "that too."

FOURTEEN

At five o'clock the following evening, George Mahbee deployed his men around the meeting place. They virtually took over all the buildings surrounding the cul-de-sac. There were men at the windows as well as on the rooftops overlooking the alley, and Mahbee felt as safe as if he were in his own office.

Leo Valniev had declined to accompany Mahbee and his men to the meeting, saying that since he was only there in an advisory capacity, it was not necessary for him to be there. He had no doubts about the outcome; he knew that whether it was Berbick who showed up, or Nick Carter, either one would be killed almost immediately.

But Valniev had a hunch, and he was going to play it out. . . .

At exactly seven o'clock, George Mahbee walked through the alley and into the cul-de-sac. He had instructed his men to turn on the lights in the buildings surrounding the fountain and to stay away from the windows so that they couldn't be seen. The only light in the little courtyard was the light from the windows, and as Mahbee entered, his eyes flicked about but could find no one. He looked up at the sides of the buildings and then at the rooftops, and was satisfied that he could not see any of his men. Obviously he had been the first to arrive, so he walked to the fountain and sat down to wait.

He would wait a long time.

Leo Valniev approached the Presidential Building warily, and as he had suspected, the guards that were usually at the front entrance had been removed. Mahbee had taken as many men as he could spare with him to the meeting, leaving the Presidential Building unguarded.

Valniev entered the building with his gun in hand. There were three floors and many governmental offices in the building, but he felt that the action would be on the top floor, where the president's office and living quarters were.

He took the stairs, being careful not to make any noise as he ascended to the third floor. The building was as quiet as death, but he could feel someone's presence. He was certain that if there was going to be a meeting that night, this was where it was going to take place.

He wondered idly how Mahbee was feeling, sitting in that cul-de-sac all alone. . . .

● ● ●

Mahbee was seething, and by nine o'clock he was boiling with rage, his anger directed in many different directions.

He was furious with his men. For no one to show up, one of them had to have gotten careless and allowed himself to be seen. Berbick—or whoever was supposed to meet with him—had probably sensed a trap and abandoned the meeting.

There was also Leo Valniev, who must have known that something like this would happen. Why else would he stay behind? He had allowed Mahbee to come here and be made a fool of, and for that he would pay.

A lot of people would pay for this indignity . . . but he decided to wait another half hour, just in case. . . .

Jules Berbick was sleeping at that moment, and Liza Berbick was sitting at his bedside, holding her father's gun and keeping her eyes on the entrance.

Where are you, Nick? she kept thinking. *When will you come?*

Valniev was on the third floor now, and it was still as quiet as the grave. There were two main offices, the president's and his assistant's—and then there was the vice-president's office. On the other side of the floor was the president's living quarters.

Where would Nick Carter hide himself? he wondered. *In an office or in the apartment?*

When Mahbee returned—and he would return angry—he would probably head straight for his office, surrounded by his men, barking orders and looking to make someone pay for the hours he had spent waiting by that dry fountain. . . .

Valniev's eyes slid to the door of the presidential apartment, Mahbee's current residence. That was where Mahbee would be found alone; that was where Valniev would hide, waiting for Mahbee to come to him, alone and unprotected.

Was Nick Carter really going to become an assassin for his country? Valniev did not think that was like him. Oh, he knew that Carter had killed before, but there was nothing in his file that said that he had ever killed in cold blood.

What else could his plan be, though? Berbick and his people—if indeed it was Berbick who was their leader—had no hope of defeating Mahbee and his forces, so the only way to win was to get rid of Mahbee. The idea did not exactly offend Valniev, since he did not like the man, but his country wanted what Santa Caribe had to offer, and he could not allow the American agent to kill George Mahbee.

Even if it meant killing Carter, a man he did like and, even more, respected.

As he had said to himself before, Nick Carter deserved no less than to be killed by Leo Valniev.

George Mahbee returned to the Presidential Building in a white-hot rage.

"Someone will pay!" he shouted as he climbed the stairs to the third floor, followed by his personal guard.

When they reached his office, Mahbee sat heavily at his desk, picked up his phone, realized that he had no one to call, and slammed it down viciously. The receiver bounced up and clattered to the desk top, and he picked it up and slammed it down again, keeping his hand on it this time.

"Someone will pay dearly!" he shouted again, slamming his other hand on his desk.

He looked up at the four men who comprised his personal guard and pointed his finger at them.

"I want to know who got careless!" he snapped. "I want that man in my office in less than an hour, or I will have *your* hides for *his* stupidity. Do you understand?"

"Yes, sir," one man said. "But what if no one was careless, Mr. President?"

"Get me someone!" Mahbee screamed, jumping to his feet and slamming his fists on the desk. "Draw straws, for all I care, but someone must pay! Get out, now! Get out!"

The four men filed out of the office, and two of them took up positions outside the office door.

Inside, Mahbee seethed for a few moments before deciding that there actually was someone he wanted to call. He picked up the phone and dialed the Hotel Caribe. He asked for Leo Valniev's room, but when there was no answer after a few rings he slammed the instrument down again, swearing loudly and violently.

The Russian will pay for this, he vowed to himself. He was supposed to be an advisor; he should have advised Mahbee not to go to the meeting. Instead he agreed that the meeting was a good idea, and this is what happened.

He would pay and pay dearly.

Mahbee stood up and walked to the window to look

down at the streets. He was so angry that he abandoned normal caution and was leaving himself an open target, framed in the window.

He thought back to that morning when he killed President Bili Makumbo. Could Jules Berbick still be alive? He had fired at the man and had seen the bullet go into his chest, but then the vice-president had run from the limousine and scrambled into the brush, and he and Duncan had been unable to find him anywhere.

Surely, Mahbee thought, *he must have bled to death somewhere.*

If he had somehow survived, then he was the only one who knew that Mahbee had killed Makumbo. Why hadn't he stepped forward and made that fact public? Why was the man waiting so long to expose him?

Berbick had always appeared to be a nonentity, but Mahbee had never quite accepted that. He had often thought that Berbick's bland facade might be just that—an act. On the other hand, Makumbo had been a rather obvious buffoon whose only redeeming quality was that the people loved him. Mahbee had suspected that there was someone behind Makumbo pulling the strings and putting the words into his mouth.

It had to have been Berbick!

If that was indeed the case, then Berbick was both smart and clever. He was waiting to recover from his wound, at which time he would step forward, announce himself as a candidate for the presidency, and hope that the sentimental vote would go to him. He was obviously intending to defeat Mahbee at the polls without revealing the fact that Mahbee was the assassin of President Makumbo. Then, if and when Berbick was elected, he would probably take action against Mahbee as the murderer of Santa Caribe's beloved first president.

Mahbee could not allow that; he had too many plans to allow anyone to foil them. Berbick had to be found and killed without anyone finding out, or everything that George Mahbee had worked for would be for nothing.

Mahbee was cold, chilled to the bone by both the coolness of the evening and his latest thoughts. He wanted a hot bath, a lot of brandy, and a warm woman. All of these could be had in his quarters—at least the bath and the brandy were there already. The woman would have to be sent for later, but he had his pick of women, both island girls and tourists. What woman would not want to bed down with the next president of Santa Caribe?

He walked to the door of his office and opened it, then stepped into the outer office where the two guards were standing watch.

"Accompany me to my apartment," he ordered, and they fell into step behind him. When they reached the door to his quarters he said, "Remain on guard here. I might have an errand for one of you to run."

The guards knew that this meant that Mahbee might be sending one of them for a woman.

"When the others return, summon me."

"Yes, sir," they said in unison.

Mahbee stepped into his quarters, which he looked upon as a sanctuary, and closed the door behind him. He took a deep breath and felt his muscles relax. This was the only place on the entire island where he allowed himself to unwind, where he felt almost entirely safe.

He walked to a small, portable bar and poured himself a large snifter of brandy. When he was officially elected president, he would have a large bar installed and would stock it with the finest liquors from all over the world. Also when he was president, more women would be his, also the world's finest. When he started trading with the Russians he would become a world-renowned, respected man, and Santa Caribe would become an important place in the world.

He drained the brandy from his glass and poured another, even larger drink. He took this one into the bedroom with him, where he removed his clothing and put on a bathrobe, then went to the bathroom to run a hot bath. A hot bath would do more for him than a hot shower, and he would keep the brandy bottle by the tub within easy reach.

When he returned with the bottle, the water was ready. He removed his robe and lowered himself into the steaming bath, feeling the aches and coldness drain out of him.

He poured another snifter of brandy to help combat the cold from the inside out, then another. The hot water and alcohol began to work on him, making him drowsy.

Berbick was the only obstacle in his way. Once he was dead, the Makumbo people would have nothing to fight for and would dissolve.

It was time to think about a woman. What kind would he like tonight? A nice, dark, firm island girl? Or one of those blond, soft, big-breasted tourists? He felt a tightening in his groin as he thought about the last blond tourist he had enjoyed, and that made up his mind for him. Now, if only he could work up the energy to get up and tell one of the guards to go and get him one. . . .

He made one attempt at getting out of the tub, but as the cool air struck his wet body he shivered and lowered himself back into the protective embrace of the water.

Another brandy was necessary before he tried again.

It was not until he had poured himself another and was relaxing in the tub with it in hand that the man with the gun stepped into the room.

"What—" Mahbee cried out, startled. He dropped the glass of brandy, which shattered as it struck the tiled floor.

"Better be careful getting out of that tub," Nick Carter said. "You wouldn't want to cut your feet on that glass."

FIFTEEN

Nick Carter made Mahbee get out of the tub, but he would not allow the man to put on his robe. He had learned a long time ago that being nude strips a man of more than just his clothes. It's hard to be brave when you're buck naked.

When they were standing in the bedroom, Mahbee's body began to sprout goose bumps and he started to shiver.

"You're mad," he told Carter. "My personal guards are right outside the door."

"Well then," Carter said. "I guess I'm just very lucky to be in here with you."

"You're the American."

"That's very good."

"Are you going to kill me?"

"Better and better."

"You can't!" Mahbee croaked, choking on the words. "Your country would never stand for it."

"What they don't know won't hurt them," Carter assured him.

"But—but when I am president I will sign an exclusive trade agreement with your country. That's what you want, isn't it?" Mahbee asked desperately.

"You change sides pretty quick, don't you?" Carter said.

"No, no," Mahbee cried, waving his hands about, "I was planning all along to trade with America."

"Forget it, Mahbee," Carter said. "It's over. I'm not interested in your lies."

"No, no—" Mahbee shouted again, frantically searching his brain for a way to stay alive, something to make the American keep him alive.

"Berbick!" he said quickly.

"What about him?" Carter asked.

"Is he really alive?" Mahbee asked. He was determined to keep talking, and to keep the American talking, until he could think of something.

"What do you think?"

"He wouldn't allow you to do this if he were," Mahbee said. "Not Jules."

"You and Berbick were good friends, were you?" Carter asked. "Is that what you're telling me?"

"Jules Berbick would never agree to assassinate anyone," Mahbee said. "Not even me."

"But he's not assassinating you," Carter told Mahbee, "I am."

"No, you're not, Nick," a voice said from behind him. It was a voice he recognized immediately.

"Leo," Carter said.

"Correct, my friend," Leo Valniev said. "Please, put your weapon down."

"I can't do that, Leo," Carter said, feeling annoyed with himself that he had been outmaneuvered. Then again, the fact that it had been Valniev who had done it softened the blow. Carter had enough confidence in his own abilities to know that no one else could have done it.

"If you shoot me," he went on, "I'll shoot Mahbee, and then you'll lose anyway."

"You will lose also, my friend," Valniev said. "Your country will be very embarrassed when the public finds out that an American agent assassinated the president of a small but important Caribbean country."

"They'll disavow any knowledge of me," Carter said. "You know that."

Mahbee was watching both men with desperate eyes, and his gaze kept going back to the barrel of Carter's Luger, which was still pointing at his gut.

"That will not save them embarrassment, my good friend," Valniev assured him. "You are still an American; whether they admit to sending you or not will be of no consequence. You know what people will think, regardless."

Yes, Carter knew what people would think all right: another coverup.

"Now, drop your gun to the floor, please, Nick," Valniev said. "Don't force me to kill you."

"You're going to kill me anyway, Leo," Carter reasoned. "I might as well take him with me."

"No!" Mahbee shouted, throwing his hands up in front of his face, but both men ignored him completely.

"You would not cause your country embarrassment simply out of spite, Nick," Valniev said. "That is not the way you operate. Put the gun down, my friend, I beg you."

In the end it was merely to keep things going that Carter did put down his gun. As long as he was alive there was a chance that he could turn the tables on Valniev—though he really didn't hold out much hope of being able to do so. The Russian had gotten the drop on him and was not likely to make a mistake now.

And then there was all that talk about embarrassing his country.

"You know, Leo," Carter said as he threw his gun on the bed, "in my country they call this dirty pool."

"Dirty pool?" Valniev said, trying the phrase on for size. "I like that. I will remember it. Dirty pool."

"Kill him! Kill him!" Mahbee began to shout. "I order you to kill him!"

Valniev gave Mahbee a disdainful look up and down, then said, "If I were you, Mr. Mahbee, I would go and put some clothes on."

Mahbee looked down at his nakedness, and if his skin had not been so dark, Carter swore that the man would have blushed. He turned and ran back into the bathroom, and then began to howl and jump around on one foot.

"I warned him about that glass," Carter said.

When Mahbee had bandaged his foot and gotten dressed, Valniev convinced him that the best thing to do was to take Carter to the docks and make it look as if he were killed trying to enter the country illegally.

"Wouldn't it look better if he was killed here?" Mahbee had asked. He clearly relished the idea of killing Carter right away, and doing it himself. "That way it would be obvious that he had come here to assassinate me."

"When the public reads that an American agent was killed trying to enter a foreign country illegally, and armed, they will naturally assume that he was here on a mission of assassination," Valniev explained. He spoke as if he were talking to a small child. "If we kill him here we cannot establish that he was here illegally. He could have entered as a tourist, on vacation, and decided to kill you on his own when the trouble broke out. The other way it will appear that he had been sent here by his government specifically to kill you."

In the end Mahbee agreed, but with one condition.

"Before we kill him—before I kill him—I want him to tell us where Jules Berbick is."

"Berbick is dead," Carter spoke up.

Mahbee thought a moment, then said, "I don't believe you're telling the truth."

"Neither do I," Valniev said, as much as he hated to agree with Mahbee, "but we can discuss it further when we get to the docks. Call your guards, Mahbee."

"Ha!" Mahbee said with disgust. "My guards!"

He called them and gave them a severe dressing down before giving orders to accompany him and the prisoner to the docks.

"Bring my car around," he barked to one of them,

"and find the rest of those fools. I want you all to come with us."

"Yes, sir."

As the two guards started to leave the room Mahbee shouted, "One of you stay here, for God's sake!"

"Yes, sir," they said, then looked at each other, trying to decide who should go and who should stay.

Valniev stepped forward, pointing at one and then the other. "You go and you stay."

Happy that the decision had been made for them, they each obeyed.

"What a command decision," Carter said. "Running a country's a snap, eh, Mr. President?"

"Shut up!" Mahbee shouted, spittle flying from his mouth.

Carter's expression was one of mock indignation, Valniev tried to hide a smile, and Mahbee's face was twisted and ugly with rage and humiliation.

Let's get out of here, Mahbee snapped, hoping to regain both his dignity and sense of authority. "Move, Carter!"

Mahbee and Valniev ushered Carter into the limousine, and they made it to the docks with very little trouble. Carter didn't have much of an opportunity to cause any; aside from Valniev and Mahbee, there were four guards riding with them, and they all were armed, holding their weapons in their hands. Valniev had put his gun away.

"We'll take him into the immigration office," Mahbee said. He was limping due to his cut foot, but he had once again gained control of himself and of the situation, and had forgotten how, only a short while earlier, he had been begging for his life.

They got out of the limousine and walked toward the immigration building, the four guards forming up around Carter, Mahbee and Valniev walking behind. As they approached the building, it suddenly exploded in a ball of white flame, the force of the explosion throwing them all to the ground.

Carter reacted immediately. Feeling the heat of the flames on his face, he quickly jumped one of the guards and grabbed his gun, then ran back toward the car, past Mahbee and Valniev.

"Get him, you fools!" Mahbee screamed.

Three of the guards staggered to their feet, and Mahbee and the Russian rushed from their line of fire as they sighted down on Carter's retreating back.

Carter turned in time to see them aiming at him. The gun he had picked up was a CAR-15, and he squeezed the trigger and fired half the magazine in the direction of the guards. The three men threw themselves flat, and Carter tried to locate Mahbee and Valniev.

Suddenly a group of people burst onto the docks, and Carter saw that they were led by Willem and Liza. They began to fire toward the guards, who now forgot about Carter and turned their attention to the new danger. This left Carter to take care of Mahbee and Valniev.

He spotted Mahbee right away, running in obvious panic toward the end of one of the docks, apparently unmindful of the fact that when he reached the end of it there would be no place for him to go.

Carter took one last look around for Valniev, but the

wily veteran agent seemed to have vanished.

The guards, outnumbered by Willem's small force, were retreating now, and one by one the four men were knocked over by a barrage of lead. Carter left them to Willem and Liza, and took off after Mahbee.

In the darkness he could hear Mahbee's frantic footsteps and their vibrations on the wooden dock beneath his feet. He did not run after the man, but simply walked, knowing full well that Mahbee would be waiting for him at the end of the dock—either that or he'd be swimming.

As he approached the end of the dock he began to make out the shape of Mahbee, who was turning first one way and then another, looking for somewhere to go.

There were no boats tied to this particular pier, and the man seemed very hesitant to chance the dark, choppy water. Carter wondered idly if Mahbee knew how to swim.

He could hear the sound of shots behind him, but they were gradually decreasing. Finally it was quiet except for the sound of the raging fire caused by the explosion.

Mahbee turned and saw Carter, and put his arms out in front of him as if to ward off the hail of bullets he was expecting with his upraised palms.

"No, no," he begged. He clasped his hands in front of him and fell down to his knees, crying, "No, please, no!" as Carter aimed the muzzle of the CAR-15 at him.

Enough time passed for the AXE agent to have pulled the trigger several times, but still he did not—

which was probably crueler to the blubbering man than killing him outright would have been.

Come on, Nick, he told himself, *you've killed before. It's not so hard, just pull the trigger and he'll be gone.*

"Please!" Mahbee shouted once more, and then he covered his face with both hands.

Carter's finger tightened on the trigger of the CAR-15, but still he didn't pull it.

He became aware of someone running up behind him, but instinct told him it was not someone he should worry about.

It was Willem.

"They're all dead," he told Carter, stopping next to him.

"All right."

"Mahbee is the only one left."

"What about the Russian?" Carter asked.

"He's gone," Willem said. "He must have escaped in all of the confusion."

Good, Carter thought. *See you again, Leo.*

"Mahbee is finished," Willem said, "at last."

"Yes."

"Are you going to kill him?" Willem asked.

"Yes," Carter said.

He was about to pull the trigger when Willem said, "Let me," and raised the muzzle of his M-16.

Before Carter could react, Willem had pulled the trigger on his gun, and the force of the bullets slamming into Mahbee knocked him right off the dock and into the dark water. Willem ran to the end of the dock and, obviously not yet satisfied, continued to fire into Mahbee's floundering body until it disappeared from sight.

Liza was next to Carter by then, touching his arm. "Are you all right?" she asked.

"Fine," he said, lowering the muzzle of his gun. "How about you?"

"I'm fine," she said. "Everything is fine, now."

Yes, Carter thought, *everything is fine*.

SIXTEEN

Three days later, Nick Carter was getting ready to leave Santa Caribe by more conventional means than he had used to enter the tiny country.

He had already said good-bye to Ollie the bellboy, and had tipped him generously, so when there was a knock on the door he knew it wasn't him.

It was Willem and Liza.

"We wanted to say good-bye," Liza told him, hugging him tightly.

"I'm glad you came by," Carter said, drawing them into the room. "I have some bourbon left, and some questions."

"Questions?" Willem asked.

"I'm still as in the dark now about some things as I was three days ago," Carter said.

"I will help if I can," Willem volunteered.

"Good," Carter said. "First question: Who fired at Liza and myself while we were on our way to the cave to arrange my talk with Berbick?"

Willem lowered his eyes. "I'm afraid that was me, and I'm ashamed."

"Why'd you do it?"

"I was simply trying to scare you off and keep you from meeting President Berbick. I'm afraid Liza was right about me all along. I was jealous of you and her, and I was jealous of my relationship with President Berbick."

Willem went on to explain that he had arrived at the cave after Nick and Liza had left, and he found the bodies of his dead comrades. He knew that Carter and Liza had seen them, and he felt that this would cause Carter to be even more suspicious of him.

"I have never been in such a rage," he went on, awed by the memory of it. "I went on a desperate search of the hills for the Mahbee patrol I knew had killed them. It took me much of the day and night, but I found them and killed them all." He lifted his head this time and said, "Of this I am not ashamed."

After that he had gone to the mine shaft where Jules Berbick was hiding, and he was almost shot by Liza. It took a lot of talking to convince her that he was loyal, and it had been then that he first admitted to her that foolish jealousy had clouded his thoughts and actions. In the end, it was Jules Berbick who convinced his daughter to lower her gun and allow him to enter.

"They told me of your plan to kill Mahbee. I convinced President Berbick to let me drive all of us into the city in the jeep I stole from the patrol I wiped out, because if you succeeded in killing Mahbee, he and Liza would want to put in an appearance as soon as possible to calm the people."

After hiding Berbick, Willem decided to keep an eye on the Presidential Building and keep a small force of men at hand. He wanted to be around in the event that Carter needed help, and Liza had talked Willem into letting her accompany him.

"We were watching the entrance when Mahbee and the Russian came out with you."

"Lucky for me that you did."

"We blew up the immigration building with a few grenades, giving you a chance to get clear before we started shooting."

And the rest was history.

As soon as he appeared, Jules Berbick was acknowledged as Santa Caribe's new president by virtue of the fact that he was vice-president at the time President Makumbo was killed and so was the logical successor.

President Berbick's first official act was to open the airstrip and the docks, and to allow tourists to come in or leave as they pleased. To the president's surprise, many of the vacationers chose to stay, and others flocked to the small island.

"Let's drink a toast," Liza said.

"To what?" Carter asked.

She smiled, took hold of Willem's arm possessively, and said, "To our engagement."

"That's wonderful," he said.

He only had two glasses in the room, so he gave them to the happy couple, clinked his bottle to their glasses, and said, "Good luck and much happiness."

After they drank their toast, Willem said, "I have also come to apologize to you, Mr. Carter."

"Nick."

"Nick," Willem said. "I acted very foolishly and jeopardized all of our work, and yours. I am truly sorry."

Willem extended his hand and Carter took it.

"It all worked out for the best, Willem," he told the younger man, "and that's what counts."

"Willem has a position in Father's cabinet," Liza said proudly. "Before long he will be vice-president—as long as my father remains president, that is."

"Which will be up to the people," Carter said.

"Yes," Liza said, "the people will decide."

"That is as it should be," Willem said.

"We have to go," Liza said then. "My father will soon be addressing the people in the big park just outside Caribe City."

"I hope he has enough security," Carter said, remembering how it all started.

"I will be personally supervising his security," Willem said, and Liza beamed proudly.

"Then I have no doubts about his safety," Carter said. "I would like to attend, but I have a plane to catch. I'm due back in Washington."

"Ah, yes," Willem said, and he reached into his jacket pocket. "President Berbick asked me to give this to you," he said, handing Carter a letter-sized brown envelope.

"What is it?" Carter asked.

"It is an unofficial trade agreement," Willem said. "The president has signed it, and it assures the United States of special trade relations with Santa Caribe."

Carter scanned the letter quickly, and Willem asked, "Will it do until your country can send someone with an official document?"

"It will do very nicely," Carter assured him. "Tell President Berbick I said thank you—and congratulations on the newest addition to his family."

"Good-bye, Nick," Liza said.

"Do I get to kiss the bride?" he asked both of them.

For an answer Liza stepped forward and kissed him warmly on the mouth.

"Good-bye," he said to both of them, and they left.

Carter was ready to go almost immediately, since he was leaving all of the clothing in the room behind. He was on his way to the door when there was another knock.

It was Megan Ward, and on either side of her on the floor stood a suitcase.

"Well, where are you off to?" Carter asked. "Another island to finish your vacation?"

She made a face at him and said, "I've had my fill of islands, Nick. I thought that since you were flying back today, maybe we could fly back together." She waved a colorful folder and said, "I already bought my own ticket."

"Really?" he asked. "How can I say no to a woman who buys her own ticket?"

"You can't."

Carter picked up her bags for her, then asked, "Are you sure you're not just looking for someone to carry your bags?"

"Actually," she said, slipping her arm through one

of his, "you're absolutely right. I am looking for someone to carry my bags." She put her lips to his ear and added, "Right to my bedroom."

Nick Carter was only too happy to volunteer.

DON'T MISS THE NEXT NEW NICK CARTER SPY THRILLER

THE ALGARVE AFFAIR

Beneath the window, Carter reached up and ruffled the burlap. The movement was answered immediately by another crack from the rifle and a shower of cement chips.

"Gimme my Luger," Carter said, turning to Leonita. "And take this!"

He passed her the .45, and reloaded Wilhelmina.

"This is the trigger, this is the muzzle. You squeeze this and point this, not necessarily in that order. Got it?"

She nodded and Carter smiled. She was as calm and cool as she had been hours before, standing in a spotlight, haughtily staring out at her audience.

"One more thing . . ."

"*Sim?*"

"If they try to push that door open before I can find them, get back there, against the wall in a crouch. Hold the gun with both hands, like this."

"I understand."

"Aim for the gut, right in the middle, and keep firing until nothing moves. Got that?"

"They killed Jorge," she calmly replied. "It will be nothing to kill them."

Carter knew she meant it.

The wires inside Carter's body grew taut as he again exposed his upper body at the window and then heaved himself through. He landed on the mossy ground below like a cat, moving.

Forty yards into the woods, he started his flanking movement. He ran in a zigzag pattern twenty yards at a time, and then stopped to listen. Twice the rifle cracked from the woods in front of the house, telling him that Leonita was doing her job.

On the fifth such move, when he was about midway around the long half-circle that would take him to the sniper's position, he heard the .45 answer the rifleman's fire.

And then he heard something else: movement through the trees about fifty yards in front of him.

So, Carter thought, there are more than one of them.

He slid his hand under the pea jacket, withdrew Wilhelmina, and settled down behind a large oak to wait.

The wind was nil now, allowing him to hear every step as the second shooter approached. When Carter was sure that there was only one, he replaced Wilhelmina in his right hand with Hugo.

The thin, boned hilt was barely nestled in his palm when a short, barrel-chested man with a wide, flat face that looked like someone had stepped on it too many times burst through a tangle of vines.

He was only three feet from the oak when Carter rolled around it from the man's blind side. He came up, in an underhand swing, with the stiletto. His intention was to gut-stab the man, and then chop his windpipe with his free hand to choke off any cry.

He was a beat too late.

The man side-stepped Carter's thrust with alarming agility for one with such a short, compact body. At the same time he swung both hands as one, his clenched fists catching Carter on the back of his right elbow. If Carter hadn't followed through, high, on his swing, the blow could have broken his arm.

As it was, Hugo slipped from Carter's grasp and the force of the blow spun him around twice before his back slammed against a tree.

Like a gorilla—crouched, his arms low—the man came for Carter. Just before they came together, his right hand dived into his boot, coming up with a blade of his own.

But Carter was ready . . .

—From *The Algarve Affair*
A New Nick Carter Spy Thriller
From Charter in February

☐ 14217-6	**THE DEATH DEALER**	$2.50
☐ 14172-2	**THE DEATH STAR AFFAIR**	$2.50
☐ 14221-4	**THE DECOY HIT**	$2.50
☐ 17014-5	**THE DUBROVNIK MASSACRE**	$2.25
☐ 18102-3	**EARTHFIRE NORTH**	$2.50
☐ 29782-X	**THE GOLDEN BULL**	$2.25
☐ 33068-1	**HIDE AND GO DIE**	$2.50
☐ 34909-9	**THE HUMAN TIME BOMB**	$2.25
☐ 37484-0	**THE INSTABUL DECISION**	$2.50
☐ 47183-8	**THE LAST SUMARAI**	$2.50
☐ 58866-2	**NORWEGIAN TYPHOON**	$2.50
☐ 65176-3	**THE PARISIAN AFFAIR**	$2.50
☐ 71133-2	**THE REDOLMO AFFAIR**	$1.95
☐ 71228-2	**THE REICH FOUR**	$1.95
☐ 95305-0	**THE YUKON TARGET**	$2.50
☐ 08374-9	**THE BUDAPEST RUN #183**	$2.50

Bestselling Books

☐ 21889-X	**EXPANDED UNIVERSE,** Robert A. Heinlein	$3.95
☐ 47809-3	**THE LEFT HAND OF DARKNESS,** Ursala K. LeGuin	$2.95
☐ 48519-7	**LIVE LONGER NOW,** Jon. N. Leonard, J. L. Hofer and N. Pritikin	$3.50
☐ 80581-7	**THIEVES WORLD,** Robert Lynn Asprin, Ed.	$2.95
☐ 02884-5	**ARCHANGEL,** Gerald Seymour	$3.50
☐ 08933-X	**BUSHIDO,** Beresford Osborne	$3.50
☐ 08950-X	**THE BUTCHER BOY,** Thomas Perry	$3.50
☐ 09231-4	**CASHING IN,** Antonia Gowar	$3.50
☐ 87127-5	**WALK ON GLASS,** Lisa Robinson	$3.50
☐ 78035-0	**STAR COLONY,** Keith Laumer	$2.95

Available at your local bookstore or return this form to:

CHARTER BOOKS
Book Mailing Service
P.O. Box 690, Rockville Centre, NY 11571

Please send me the titles checked above. I enclose _____ Include 75¢ for postage and handling if one book is ordered; 25¢ per book for two or more not to exceed $1.75. California, Illinois, New York and Tennessee residents please add sales tax.

NAME_____

ADDRESS_____

CITY_____STATE/ZIP_____

(allow six weeks for delivery)